DRUMSHANBO

3rd edition with emendations as highlighted by the sharp eyes of Terry Gray and Michael Smith. Many thanks.

First published in 2021
by Iron Mountain Press
18 Quaker Rd.,
Cork, Ireland.

Typesetting and Cover Design:
FlintlockCovers.com

ISBN 978-1-3999-0151-2

DRUMSHANBO

CONOR MC MANUS

IRON MOUNTAIN PRESS

ACKNOWLEDGEMENTS

The first six stories in this collection were funded and published as a collection by a bursary from Roscommon County Council and Three Spires Press respectively, and published individually by Crannog and The Moth literary magazines.

Grateful thanks are due to Monica Corish, Gerry Boland and Aine Butler (Roscommon County Council) for enabling and facilitating publication of some of these pieces in The Leitrim Observer and The Roscommon Herald.

To Leitrim County Council for a bursary for the Tyrone Guthrie centre where I wrote and early draft of this book.

To O'Bheal (a poetry event and open mic, in Cork City) and all its attendees upon whom I have inflicted several of these stories in a Leitrim accent and without whose positive response none would ever have seen the light of day.

To friends who have critiqued and encouraged and Colm Scully who gave the final read.

To my brother Patrick who accidentally fell into the role of Chief Distribution Officer for the book and kept shelves stocked. It's very much appreciated.

Finally, to Dermot Mc Partland, Mc P, a townie, whom I met shortly after we both arrived in Drumshanbo with much ado, and who was still there to advise me on the publication of this book, fifty four years later.

For my mother and father, whose humour, wit and turns of phrase are at the heart of this book.

CONTENTS

PROLOGUE

The town was set in the crook of the river beneath the rookery. A town I knew every nook and cranny of, every twist and turn of, every dip and hollow of. Willie wagtails hung out and swifts soared high above the town on summer's evenings. A copper beech, a lime and two cherry blossoms lined the High Street and laid down a carpet of petals that softened the concrete each April. There were thirteen pubs in all. Six of them lined up door to door on High Street. Two were also grocery shops and one was a tailors and on Mill Hill there was a woman's drapery with a bottle of Powers in the window among the women's apparel. There were three butchers, two chemists, two supermarkets, two hardwares, an assortment of odd shops including two draperies and men's outfitters, three hairdressers and two barbers, including Larry Welch. There was an old school, a new school, a well and three men with one bad leg each. One sweet-shop come chip shop, one private kitchen come chip-shop. A tech and two priests' houses. Two priests, four guards, a Methodist parson. Three churches and a house for the parson. There was a convent with nuns in, a boxing club, a football pitch, a burnt out old bakery and a disused cinema.

The Market Yard had run-down sheds that housed slot machines and table football and swing boats outside. I remember the taking down of the sheds, with my father and the taking off of the slates. I found a dudgeen on the wall plate with a harp and shamrocks and Erin go Bragh raised on it.

It must have been 1976, the year Jimmy Nugent went to England. I remember we were doing up the Market Yard house and there was an old pedal motorbike in it with the tyres perished on it. Jimmy took it to go in and out to home on until both tyres were flittered. But even before that, Junior Mc Gowan started his Volkswagen garage there and before that there was Mickey English blacksmith who made our tongs and who I don't remember, but I heard The Captain talk about him. There was one dump and two slaughter houses. There was Corryard, the Burma, Bakery Hill and Carrig na Breac. It was once a town full of kids; Mulveys, Grays, Herons, Kanes, Morans, Scollans, Byrnes, Fitzgeralds, Mc Hughs, all strong names, strong people. People whom after forty years, and away for much of it, I can still recognise them by the backs of their heads. Warm people. Open people. My people.

The bog brown river flows from Derry Hallow lake and out across the flatlands that sweep to the mountain. It cuts under the Narrow Gauge at Shane Mc Keon's rhubarb patch and on it flows. Behind Jim Kane's slaughter house and by the Rock Well, along the vegetable gardens at the foot of Dristernan and on into the town. It continues under Tom Mc Girl's bridge at the bottom of the Hilly Road where the great chestnut tree grows. It slips gently along behind Tony Mc Gowan's and across under the road at the Gunner McGee's tin hut. It runs on behind Tom Joe Macs, Crawford's, the Bank, the Market Yard and on towards the mill race at the jam factory in Carricknabrack, before flowing round the fair green and on towards Lough Allen. It skirts the town along the bottom of the Market Yard. It's neither deep nor wide, though we thought it was deep and wide. A footbridge made from railway tracks traversed it at the back of Tom Joe Mc's. There was a pipe across at the bank, and there was another, larger one, at the back of Campbell's Hardware. There were stepping stones you could access from the back of Patsy Canning's onto the fair green. The green was where the circus and amusements and bonfires were held and where the rock with the hole in it for the cure for warts was, and where my father once played with the twin Mc Partlands and his little brother Terney.

Generations of crows have looked down on us forever and of an evening they'd swirl around the tops of the trees at the back of the house. A crow picking thatch off the ridge of our house could observe our back yard with one eye and the public street with the other. From high up on their perch, they could spy on the nuns gardening, in through Father Duignan's back window, down on the school, down on the club house, down on all the pubs backyards, vegetable gardens, ramshackle green houses, clothes lines and ash pits. My father would take pot shots at the crows pecking at the thatch. I don't think he believed that it would stop them, and he respected them as an enemy.

1

THE CAPTAIN—THE GUN—THE POTATO—THE RAT

One morning my mother was looking out over Tom Flynn's shoulder into the sunlit yard and wishing she was a daisy when she spotted a rat wrestling with a potato from Darwin's bowl. Darwin was our liver marked pointer and he was as old as I was. The rat was dragging the potato towards a hole in the boundary wall, beside the stack of timber, and back into the neighbours. We were watching the rat, with his pearl-black eye, tugging the potato toward the hole, when The Captain reluctantly left his breakfast, grumbling.

—Me good rat, I'll sort him out, The Captain said.

—At least he's not one of ours, my mother said trying to calm him.

I knew it annoyed The Captain having to leave the table because I knew he always enjoyed the last bit of the breakfast. He put the last bit of bacon, the last bit of egg and the last bit of boxty on the fork and used it to wipe clean the chef sauce and remaining black crispy bits off the plate and wash it all down with a fresh drop of tea. He always et the bacon rind too, and he'd even take mine if I didn't want it and he'd eat it and say it was the nicest bit. But he didn't go out the back after the rat like I thought he would. No, he went upstairs and was back in a minute with the gun, which was kept on top of the coat hooks on the landing. I'd never seen him move so fast.

When he saw the gun, Tom Flynn finished his tea with a gulp and placing the mug on the table said, Now, that's the boyo that'll sort him out.

The Captain reached for the box of cartridges stashed on top of the press over the sink. He thought they were safe there but he didn't know I could step up on the low cill and get onto the sink and get at them if I wanted too. I thought about his breakfast going cold because I hated cold boxty and I knew he hated it too.

We watched the rat drag the potato to within feet of the hole. He kept stopping and running back to the hole and coming out again and dragging it another bit and darting back to the hole again. Tom Flynn said, He can't make up his mind whether to eat his fill in the middle of the yard, there and then, or drag the whole thing away and eat it later.

The Captain pressed the two orange brass topped cartridges into the barrels with his thumb and closed the gun quietly. He told me to knock off Maurice O'Doherty. He told my mother to hold back the net curtain. He got down on one knee and asked me to bring him the milk jug off the table. My mother raised the net curtain and we could see Mister Rat making his way to the potato again. Dragging his tail he scurried and humped, scurried and humped, scurried and humped. He tugged at it and nibbled at it and rose up on his back legs with his black pearl eye watching everything and then darted back into his hole again.

The Captain told my mother to lift the window. She tried but it was stuck with paint and had to use her two hands and then the rat appeared and the window lifted with a pop and the rat scurried back to his hole. The Captain cursed. Now he was annoyed because the rat mightn't appear more, but when the window was up far enough he positioned the milk jug to hold it there. I didn't know where he was going with the jug but I looked at my mother and she shrugged me the go-ahead. I knew by the way she did it though that she didn't know what it was for either. That was one thing about The Captain, you never knew what he was going to do until he did it. Now, The Captain stuck the two barrels out through the narrow opening and raised the gun to his shoulder slowly.

I pulled the chair out into the middle of the floor to look out over him and he said shush and my mother tried to talk and he said shush again.

I knew my mother was annoyed with him being annoyed and I knew then we had a situation—him down on one knee with the gun at his shoulder looking at the potato beside the timber stack, me standing on the chair looking at the potato beside the timber stack and not able to move without him shushing, my mother holding up the net curtain and giving me eyes and looking at the ceiling, and Tom Flynn sitting with his legs crossed, watching us and not saying a word.

I knew he'd get the rat because he shot two crows off of Tom Joe Mac's BBC aerial with the one shot. And that wasn't easy because Healy's was the other side of Low Street. He stood in our gateway so no one would see him and fired and the two crows tumbled down the roof and fell the three stories, landing on the footpath outside Tom Joe's shop door with a soft plop. He sent me over to get the two crows and put them in the dustbin.

The rat took it's time at coming back out. The Captain

adjusted himself on the floor again and sat back on his heel like a real sniper. All we had to do was wait.

I knew fellas that went shooting rats in the dump or in behind Kilraine's slaughterhouse, in the gut barrels—the rats loved it and there was no shortage of them.

I was getting tired standing on the chair and I was sorry I ever pulled it out. I moved on the chair and The Captain said shush again and I began to think this thing with the rat could go on forever. I knew The Captain, and I knew he could wait for up to three days, easily. Me standing on the chair not able to move without him shushing, him on the floor not wanting to move looking at the potato beside the timber stack and my mother holding up the curtain and looking at the ceiling. The boxty and rasher were still on the table if only we could get to them. I had to go to school but now that didn't seem to be important. I was saying nothing.

Then a shot reverberated round the kitchen and through the house. It was the loudest thing I'd ever heard and I wasn't expecting it because the rat wasn't near the potato. My mother said, You got the effer, because she didn't like them round the place at all, even if it wasn't one of ours. Tom Flynn said, That's the last he'll eat. And my mother said, We'll make a fresh pot of tea and she went and put the kettle on.

The Captain opened the gun and took out the empty cartridge and I could see the blue smoke rising from the barrel and the smell stung in my nostrils. He had only fired once and gave me the gun and the empty shell and he held onto the full one and put it back in the box on the press over the sink that I could get at if I wanted to. I smelt the empty shell and watched the smoke come out of it.

Through the window, I could see my mother already crossing the yard to the dustbin with me bould rat arched on the end of the thongs. My mother came in and she was still talking about it. She was proud of The Captain.

—That was one rat that didn't know what hit him. Well, it was the quickest thing. He just stuck his nose out and bang, she said, clapping her hands. I thought then that The Captain might have been telling the truth about himself and Audey Murphy being snipers with the LDF. But that was The Captain, he was always one step ahead of me, I was watching the potato while he was watching the hole.

2

HOOKS, PLIERS AND DISGORGERS—SHOOTING PIKE—A SCIENCE AND AN ART—BAG OF PUPS—BALLYFARNON

Every September English fishermen, burly bucks from the coalmines of Yorkshire, came for fresh air and I was freed from the master and the Irish and his quick questions. In the back of a station wagon, jammed with tackle and jammed between two miners that talked liked a prayer book and ate cheese and onion sandwiches, I headed off to Killeshandra for the day.

All the men had three fishing rods, and six rod rests, and ten quiver tips, and fifty floats, and a hundred hooks, and pliers, and disgorgers, and keep nets, and landing nets, and lead weights, and real catapults, for firing a handful of maggots out to where the float was to set the bream mad. And chicken feed for the fish, and flasks of tea, and sandwiches, and umbrellas. Everything had to be tramped through gates and over styles and across fields of waist high wet rushes, wet coats and waders flailing, to the fishing spot. There they set me up with a rod that was twice my size and showed me how to tie on a fish hook and hook on maggots so they didn't burst, and set a float, and catch rud and roach and perch and bream, that we threw back.

Once I caught an eel and I wasn't supposed to catch an eel and he tangled everything, but I brought him home with the hook still in him and my Mother said she wouldn't cook it because they wriggled on the pan even if you cut the head off. She said, Bring it down there to Joe Ganley, he'll eat it. And I did, and Joe was delighted with it. I noticed he had YR sauce out on the table and I thought that my mother was right, He'd eat anything that fella. And I didn't know how she knew Joe Ganley would eat eels.

Weights and Measures said, Fishing is a science and an art, there was that much to learn. And he was right. How do you know where to set the float on the line so the hook is at the right depth? How do you know how many of the little lead balls do you clamp on the line to get the float to stay upright in the water? And how do you know when to use a float and when to use a bomb? It was a science, an art. A bomb was a pear-shaped lead weight with a wire eye in it. How would you know by looking at the lake that the fishing would be good? And a bream; big, fat, flat, and yellow bellied like the pup that died from chicken bones, was easy enough to recognise but how could you tell the difference between a rud, a roach and a perch? It was a science. And I learned to tie a fisherman's knot that was like a hangman's noose on the tiniest of hooks—the number nineteen and it wasn't even the smallest. And these miners with fingers like sausages and them tying on the delicate hook. And to get two maggots to dangle on that hook without bursting them—Weights and Measures was right, it was a science and an art.

And they had a scales for weighing the big one when you caught him. And what if you caught a pike? Would he pull you in? But these boys didn't fish for pike, it was the Northern boys went for the pike. Down at the weekends, down for pike, down from Hollywood and Bangor, with names like Roy and Big Alec, the Protestants took their pike by day and the Provos took everything else by night—bream, rud, roach and perch to sell in London's fancy restaurants or maybe for cat and dog food. Same difference, somebody said. And they burned a bus belonging to English fishermen in Ballinamore. Everyone knows who done it. That was the sort of the Ballinamores. And they threatened Fr. Tighe, the curate, who was out on the lake with a shotgun and a flash lamp trying to stop them. But Fr. Tighe had a tooth missing for holding his pipe and he could talk and smoke at the same time and spent years out foreign and he wasn't afraid. And he denounced them from the altar for the netting and said they'd clean out the lake and that they were getting help from locals. And I wondered who the locals were.

But uncle Gerald who came from America had no interest in maggots or chicken feed. He chewed gum, said the worm was your only man and drove into Carrick to buy a tin of worms off of the tinkers on the marina for a pound. A penny a worm they said. There's a hundert worms in the tin, Sir. How he could come from America and know to buy worms off the tinkers on the marina I never knew. I never heard of such a thing and I lived there all my life. And uncle Gerald just had the one rod and it was a short one and he could put it in the car already set up and he had spare hooks and weights in little plastic pouches in his pocket. And he wasn't going to tramp a half a mile through wet rushes and mucky gaps to get to a lake when you could fish there and then off the marina in white shorts and white runners and white tee-shirt. And you didn't have to be out for the whole day sitting on a basket and eating sandwiches and catching cold, and he didn't bother with floats or chicken feed and just bomb-fished all the time. And he didn't care what he caught. And if a fish got away he'd inspect the half a worm in the palm of his hand and laugh and chew his gum and call out across the Shannon to the fish, You little cocksucker's. And he didn't bother with umbrellas either. If it rained you could just sit into the car until it cleared or drive up the town of Carrick spotting the Germans in their big yellow raincoats and yellow wellingtons and he said, You can always tell the tourists in Ireland, they're the ones wearing the raincoats.

I was telling Molloy about the raincoats and he said the Germans were taking all the pike back to Germany and cleaning out the lake. They could pay for their holiday with them. The Germans liked their pike. But nobody I knew, well except maybe Joe Ganley who'd eat YR sauce and eels, would eat pike because they were dirty things and they ate rubbish and rats and pregnant terriers.

I knew Joe Ganley shot pike alright, because he was in our house drinking hot brandy on Stephens day with his gun and belt of cartridges left by the fire and I wanted rid of him because I was afraid they would explode and the whole house would go up with the thatched roof and I thought I'd have to bar him from coming in with his gun and cartridges. He said he was shooting pike when they came in, big and fat, into the reeds to spawn. Or to eat bags of pups, I thought. That's what you did with pups you didn't want or maybe kittens you didn't want—put them in a bag and throw them across the bridge at the Galley into the Shannon. And if a stray dog walked into your yard and you couldn't get rid of it you put him in the boot and brought him to Ballyfarnon and let him out there. Ballyfarnon's in Roscommon.

It was then I knew Father Tighe had his hands full and his work cut out for him with the Provos and the Germans trying to make sure there'd be enough pike and perch for the Miners and the Protestants. Because the miners and the Protestants drank a few pints and spent a few pound, not like the Germans who brought their beer and food from Germany and annoyed everyone because they supped all night from one glass of Guinness between two and annoyed the local musicians with bad bodhran playing. They didn't have the nhyagh and that was worse than the hippies with their guitars and leather wristbands or the Americans looking for ice.

3

UNCONSCIOUS FROM DRINK—PARNELL, CORNEY AND THE ANTI-PARNELLITES—OUT AND OUT PROVOS—LEPRECHAUN SUITS

He's like Jesus Christ on the cross, my mother said, when she found Donie Byrne, unconscious from drink, with his arms outstretched on the carpet of our Good Room floor. He slept on his back with his head under the sink. He wore a beard, his hair long, a brown t-shirt, and nothing else. My Mother said, He might look like a hippy but he had a good pensionable job in the motor tax in Dublin and he was a great flute player. I went in for a look and was embarrassed with my mother standing there and him with his bits out. But she was laughing and said, Imagine that thing going into an office like that on a Monday morning.

The Good Room's open fire had a high mantelpiece upon which sat two porcelain dogs, a baby grandfather clock from America, and a picture of my uncle on my mother's side who picked potatoes with Big Tom on Jersey Island before he went to sea and before Big Tom was Big Tom.

On one wall hung a picture of Pope John the Twenty Third. Beside it, a black and white photo of my mother, The Captain and the Bishop of Darwin Australia, The Captain's cousin, on their wedding day.

On the opposite wall, over a side board with a set of silver which The Captain's grandfather got on his retirement from the board of the Cavan/Leitrim railway hung a signed picture of Charles Stewart Parnell—the uncrowned king of Ireland. The railway was long gone—the tracks cut up to make gateposts and hay sheds and the engine sent to India. Weights and Measures said it would take a good man six hours to cut through a railway track with a hacksaw.

My great-grandfather did jail for Parnell. And The Captain had a paper clipping that called him 'a Drumshanbo corner boy' after him and his brother Corney, who ended up shot in America, had a fight with the priests and the Anti-Parnellites in Carrick and broke up the rally and ran Tim Healy, Parnell's enemy, out of town. That's what you called people that were against something—anti this or anti that. I wondered were my great-grandfather and his brother like the boot boys on Hill Sixteen with their denim jackets and red monkey boots with yellow lacers—fighting when Dublin lost.

Once a year The Captain's cousins, two brothers, The Pipe and The Priest, would visit and they'd keep The Captain up half the night drinking whiskey and talking about Parnell.

The Pipe was a teacher who chewed the pipe and drank tea and knew how to make a poultice for the warble. The Priest was from Alabama with no collar and the top button of his black shirt open. He drank whiskey and smoked all-white cigarettes that looked long in his hand. He was the priest for them out there on death row and said they called the electric chair The Yellow Mama and you could be on death row waiting to die for ten years. And he asked me questions about school and would I be going away to school and I didn't know what he was talking about.

One night I was listening to them talk and The Pipe said,

Tim Healy was a pure bastard. His face was tight and the pipe moved up and down and I'd seen his teeth when he said it. That was the first time I heard anybody curse in front of a priest and I thought you couldn't do that. I looked at the Priest and he had a serious face and was nodding in agreement with The Pipe—not at all put out by the curse word. I looked at The Captain and he was nodding and agreeing with a serious face and I was trying to calculate how long Tim Healy was dead and did they know him. Nobody was saying anything and I felt I should say something but I knew it would be a danger to say something like, Poor Tim Healy, for instance, even as a joke. I knew I had to be careful in these situations. I had been in trouble the Monday before with Jack Carty for opening my mouth.

Jack Carty worked in Campbell's Hardware and he was all chat if I went in looking for a tap washer say, or brass butt hinges maybe, or heavy-duty sticky-backed tape to redo the joint in the lino on the bar floor. Pulling the bottle-green tape quickly off the roll, he'd use the length of his arm to measure it. He said, It was one yard, or thirty-six inches exactly, from his thumb to his oxter, a perfect specimen of a man. My mother said, He isn't a bad so and so but he's an out and out Provo.

The Embassy had been burned the previous Saturday in Dublin and I was in the shop and Jack was giving out about the guards beating up the protestors and he said, The Guards caused the riot, and Pat Deasy and Jim Noonan were in looking for a bag of cement and a pound of inch and a half ovals and not saying much. Just things like, Ah shur you couldn't be up to them, and, You'd have to be up early to catch a Guard, ha, ha, ha, and I just said, The protestors had metal pipes wrapped in barbed wire and covered with black flags. Jack lit on me. Where the fuck did you hear that shite, he said. I'd never heard him curse or talk to me like that before but his face was red. I said it was on the news. I had seen it on the television. And then he blew a gasket completely and said, More fuckin' lies from those Sticky cunts above in Donnybrook. I didn't know what he meant by that but I knew from then on that sometimes you had to be careful with what you said and I knew this was one of those times. So I wasn't going to say anything, good, bad nor indifferent about Tim Healy, dead or alive. I just nodded and looked serious.

And it was in our Good Room where Sean Mac Diarmada held a meeting and spoke when he came to rouse the people of Drumshanbo and light the flame of freedom in Leitrim, but they weren't too happy with that and they pushed him off the High Street wall and him with the bad leg. I think I was the only person in my class that knew Sean Mac Diarmada had a bad leg. I felt proud that Sean Mc Diarmada was in the history book and him from Leitrim and having been in my house. And I knew Weights and Measures was proud of him as well, Sur' wasn't he from on'y down the road, one of our own, a neighbours child. Mc Dermot was the warrior, he said, and him with yon bad leg. The only thing that put a halt to his gallop was the King's bullet. Weights and Measures dragged deep on his woodbine and blew out and down over his bottom lip creating a fan of smoke. He reached for his rum and black off the counter and looked into it, swirling it in the glass he said gravely, before gulping and grimacing, He was the same age as Our Lord when he died.

We really only used the Good Room at Christmas when we moved in the television and lit the fire in it. The rest of the year Con Ryan, a boarder from Lanesborough who stole Tippex and big elastic bands out of the bank for me, ate his breakfast and dinner in it. I don't know if Con Ryan spotted the silver snail trails across the carpet when he came down for breakfast. He must have, but he never said a haet.

On Thursday nights a dentist from Enniskillen used the Good Room to pull teeth locally. He had a diamond ring on his pinky and a gold tooth and oiled his hair and always had a few half-ones before his first customer. That's why The Captain plumbed the sink in the corner of the Good Room in the first place. And during the festival our Good Room was used to store the amplification, the mics and the speakers and stuff, and Foster and Allen used it to change into their leprechaun suits when they were playing on stage on the High Street. Apart from that we didn't use it much. So how Donie Byrne ended up on the carpet of the Good Room floor with his bits out I don't know, but it was only then I realised, anything was liable to happen in our house on the night of the Connaught Fleadh.

4

THE USELESS LUG OF A LABRADOR—WARM THE BODHRAN—OH, GRACE—HEADS AND HANDS—AWKWARD BASTARD—ROAST LAMB—LIKE A GOAT 'ATIN' CABBAGE

After Mass somebody's golden retriever with a brown collar was jumping up at the window in the kitchen, trying to eat a bluebottle. Growling, with head lowered, the dog would step back, then pounce at the window open mouthed. With his paws on the low cill he'd snap sideways at the fly buzzing and banging off the glass. Music was coming from the front bar and the potatoes were boiling on the back ring.

Pat Gilmartin was standing at the cooker with a cigarette dangling from his mouth, bodhran in hand. He wore a black leather waistcoat, black beard and black glasses. He moved the carrots off to one side to warm the bodhran. He was leaning back and squinting to avoid the smoke, breathing through the corner of his mouth and blowing the smoke away from his eyes with forced-air from flared nostrils. Holding the bodhran upside down he rubbed the goatskin in circular motion while warming it over the flame. The frustrated Labrador barked up at the fly. Spews of steam lifted and dropped the lid off the potatoes. Steam was condensing on the window. The bar was jammed.

In the bar the musicians sat under the window with a table covered with full and empty glasses in front of them and banged out, The Chickens Gone To Scotland. Ashtrays overflowed and a fog of smoke clung to the ceiling. The two brothers and the protestant stood with elbows on the high counter at one end—their usual spot. The brother with the waistcoat and the hat had left in rhubarb during the week. An old man with black-rimmed glasses and a black coat sat on a high stool with his back to the wall drinking whiskey at the other end—his usual spot. He left mass early to be the first in. In between, heads and hands clamoured for stout and chatted and shouted over the music. John Mulvey stood pressed with his back to the door gripping his pint tight to his chest. The Welt was itching to sing and the Tinker with the cravat and polio limp waited for his turn to play the tin whistle.

Behind the bar pounds were taken, the till rang and change was returned. Glasses were ploshed and washed in cold water on the spot and reused. Pints were lined up in a row, ready for the heads to be put on them, and steam rose from the boiling kettle for the awkward bastard at the hatch that wanted a hot whiskey.

—It's the middle of June.

—It's for herself, she's not a hundert.

—That aul' summer cauld is hard shook.

—Jaysus wept.

Empty glasses clinked as they were collected by handfuls and full bottles sighed as their caps were prised off. The optics gurgled and a blue beer cooler beneath the counter on a beer crate in a tangle of pipes hummed to the demand. An old laundry basket filled steadily with empty bottles that clinked as they were dropped in on top of other. The old man goaded his son-in-law with round cheeks to sing and the son-in-law started to sing a love song.

As we gather in the chapel here in old Kilmainham
Gaol,
I think about these past few weeks, oh will they say
we've failed.

People jostled and stretched and turned to see the singer and those who didn't or were too short waited patiently listening. And the volume of the chatter dropped and there was the sound of someone slowly gulping their first fresh mouthfuls.

From our schooldays they have told us We must
yearn for liberty
Yet all I want in this dark place is to have you here
with me.

Someone gave out a scolding shush to kill the final mumbles of intense conversation of the cheek-to-cheek brothers discussing the merits of a mare they wanted to buy. They both chuckled the same way and went beefy red behind their pints. The glass washing and till ringing stopped and pints were supped quietly or not supped at all.

Oh Grace just hold me in your arms and let this
moment linger,
They'll take me out at dawn and I will die.
With all my love I place this wedding ring upon
your finger,
There won't be time to share our love for we must
say goodbye.

John Mulvey straightened himself, lowered his pint, closed his eyes, put out his chest and his neck tingled as the singers voice lowered.

Now I know it's hard for you my love to ever
understand,
The love I bear for these brave men, my love for this
dear land.

Others blew, slowly upward, long draughts of smoke and vacantly watched as it swirled and began to fray. Some looked studiously downward or took extra long to crush under sole a cigarette butt. And some just picked an imaginary spot on the ceiling and stood savouring every word. And in the stillness, my mother snuck away to prod the roast and check the marrowfat peas, the potatoes and the carrots. Gilmartin never put the carrots back and they were only half done. That bollox and his effin bodhran. The love song wafted into the kitchen,

But when Padhraic called me to his side down in
the GPO,
I had to leave my own sick bed, to him I had to go.

She continued prodding the roast with a big timber-handled fork and the smell escaped from the oven as the big useless lug of a Labrador salivated at her shoulder. In the bar, in the silence of the song, the stout suppers could get the smell of lamb being roasted. Then there was a loud cheer and a clap as the man with the round cheeks closed his eyes, jerked his head to beat time and finish with all he could muster.

There won't be time--to share our love--forwe-
mustsay--goodbye.

He then reached for his pint and his father-in-law wiped under his glasses and blew his nose loudly with a loose handkerchief that he had pulled by one corner from his topcoat pocket. The brother with the hat went to bless himself and the musicians under the window burst fourth once more, to whoops and cheers and another applause, and the till rang and pints were gulped.

Then, Guard Ryan, in full uniform, appeared in the door glaring at the musicians to stop, but they cut straight into another faster tune, The Woman Of The House, and a loud cheer went up.

—That's the gangly fucker, that fella.

—Aye, look at the head on him. And an eye on him like a goat atin' cabbage. Ryan stood in the doorway until everyone drank up and left.

5

THE LONG YELLOW BUS—THE TINKERS CROSS AND THE DEVILS ELBOW—UP THROUGH THE FLOORBOARDS—THE LATCHHOOK—DARWIN AND PRINCE

Once I was late for school and Mrs. Flood said I was skating on thin ice and that I'd have to pull my socks up and that she had her eye on me. But I didn't take her serious. I knew well it was her that had me awake sometimes. I slept in the back bedroom over the kitchen and our kitchen ceiling wasn't like any other ceiling in any other house I knew. From below you could see the black joist and herring bone bridging and the underside of the floor boards of the back bedroom painted white and I knew people only drank in the kitchen when it was late so the Sergeant or Guard Ryan wouldn't hear them from the front street. I'd be wake at all hours with guitars playing and people laughing and Mrs. Flood singing the Rising of the Moon up through the floor boards. I also ran messages for Mrs. Flood and I knew she'd still be giving me the four pence to bring her back a packet of silvermints from Paddy Donnelly's after the lunch.

Donnelly's was at the top of the street and you could buy ice cream in a glass bowl with raspberry drizzled on it and triangular flakes standing up out of it. It was owned by Paddy Donnelly, a tall man who wore a cravat and a light moustache and played tricks with my money on the stainless steel lid of the ice-cream fridge just to annoy me. Once a year he holidayed in New York and stayed in the best of hotels, but you wouldn't think it to look at him and he had a stainless lad for marking the block of ice-cream precisely into equal portions before cutting it with a butchers knife.

They'd knocked the ball alley to build the new school and there were new children but I didn't know where any of them came from. They arrived in on a long yellow bus from places with names like Diffier, Cordaray, Aghagrania, wherever they were, or from Derrnadooey, Drumbullog, Cornacranaghy or Cornashamsoge wherever they were, and after school they all went back out home on that long yellow bus.

I couldn't imagine these places and I quizzed my mother as to where they were and I got answers like, 'up the mountain' or 'out beyond Grogan's, the other side of the Tinker's Cross'. The Tinker's Cross, now that was another one. The Tinker's Cross was like the Bermuda triangle, all sorts of things happened there—like black frost and car crashes. I didn't know what black frost was and Tom Flynn said, If it was freezing from four, it would be like a bottle, a livin' danger. And cars always seemed to breakdown or run out of petrol at the Tinker's Cross, or if you were going anywhere, you always had to take a left or take a right or go straight through the Tinker's Cross. But how was I supposed to know where Grogan's was if I didn't know where the Tinker's Cross was. I knew where the Devil's Elbow was and I asked my Mother, Was the Tinker's Cross out beside the Devil's Elbow or was it out the other road, out by the witch's house with the star on the door or was it on the way to Carrick passed the house in the trees that moved when it rained? She just said, Stop asking daft questions, and told me to get out of her sight before she crucified me. And I couldn't understand how my mother seemed to know who these children were, Dolans and Mc Governs, Clarkes and Kane's and I had never seen any of them before and I knew everyone in the town.

I was put sitting beside Michael Flood in our new grey desks and plastic chairs and bare block walls and in front of Stephanie Mc Loughlin who had long blond hair like the one out of Abba and I loved her from the minute I saw her. I loved the one out of Abba too. And Sarah Reynolds who came home from England for the summer had long blond hair and I loved her for a while as well. I remembered trying to get a look at Sarah Reynolds on the High Street one hot summer's day when Prince, our liver-marked pointer, ran out in front of a Honda fifty and was left lying in the middle of Barrack Square not able to move. The Captain had just bought him and he was a beautiful dog with big brown eyes and was speckled all over and had a big brown spot on his back the size of an Easter egg but he was young and gangly and giddy and didn't know the town. I ran for The Captain and he came and carried him down to the shed in an old top coat. That evening he brought Prince away to get the lead cure and I haven't seen him since. The Captain had bought Prince after Darwin our old pointer had died and I knew The Captain missed Darwin and was put out by seeing Prince in that state. I knew The Captain loved his dogs and his face would light up and he'd pat them and scratch their ears because they liked it and he'd talk to them, Ah, me good fella, how are you today, and I thought he liked them more than he liked people. The Captain trained him to fetch with a spit for smell on a ball of old socks. Prince was a great dog.

In Mrs. Flood's class, we had tried knitting, plain and pearl and casting off and dropping stitches and holes and knots and making scarves and hats with tassels and wool snakes, but now rug making was Mrs. Flood's latest brainwave. Mrs. Flood must have thought it was a good idea and must have thought the latch-hooks were a good idea, after all they didn't have a point and what harm could they possibly do. But she wasn't banking on Michael Flood, in from Diffier on the long yellow bus—same name no relation, as he was quick to point out.

Mrs. Flood had given us each a piece of white mesh about a foot square. And bits of wool which we'd cut with a scissors with plastic handles and rounded ends so's we wouldn't take the eyes out of other, and this latch hook. This latch hook, now, was a metal bar with a bend on the top like a fishing gaff except with a pear-shaped wooden handle. The handle was smooth and round and nice to hold and fitted comfortably in my hand. It was the same handle as was on the bradawl that The Captain used if he was fitting a hinge for a door, say. He'd chisel out a bed for the hinge and then use the sharp point of the bradawl to pierce the soft wood and make pilot holes for the screws. And if the hinge didn't fit right he'd tear up his cigarette packet and use the cardboard to shim it out. The Captain had plenty of tricks like that, old Indian tricks he called them. Anyway, we had to loop the wool around the mesh and pull it through with this hook. That worked for a good while until Michael's hook got stuck.

My own rug wasn't going so well either as I was thinking about how nice it would be to be heading out to Diffier or Cornashamshog or Cornacrannehy sitting beside Stephanie Mc Loughlin on that long yellow bus. I was never on a bus like that before. It was similar to the one that stopped outside our house on the way to Sligo and dropped in rolls of newspapers and engine parts with brown tags on them and boxes of day old chickens that I'd let run loose round the kitchen.

Then I got a tap on the shoulder and turned and Michael's hand was up in front of his cheek holding the handle of the latch-hook and the hook end was in his right eye. I could see the outline of the hook through the thin skin of the eye-lid. Michael sat there calmly holding the hook by its smooth brown handle. Mrs. Flood was over helping Jimmy Guihen with sums. Stephanie Mc Loughlin jumped up and screamed.

Mrs. Flood was great. She got the hook out by pinching the light skin of the eyelid, and holding Michael's hand in hers, gently moved the hook downwards. I didn't like eyes at the best of times but I watched the whole operation. When it was over Michael just said, It got stuck and I jerked it, but there wasn't a word more about it. If Michael's hook hadn't got stuck when it did Michael would have made a lovely rug with a sheep-dog's head on it. He had half the dogs face done when the hook got stuck. But Michael getting the hook in his eye put an end to the rug-making and to the latch-hooks. His half-a-dogs-face was left in a drawer at the back of the class and every time I seen it after I thought about our dog Prince and wondered about how The Captain never bought another dog after that.

6

THE ORANGE MAXI—THE BINMEN—GAY PARREE—JOHNNY CASH—DICKEY'S MAXI—FROST AND SNOW—KEEP HER LIT PADDY

Beer lorries, mineral lorries and the dust bin truck edged slowly up and down High Street. Ticking over. Releasing air. Wide grapes with balls on the end of the prongs filled turf from the turf wagon into jute sacks that were carried in on hunched backs and tipped in our turf shed. Joe Gibbons, with a pencil thin moustache and hounds tooth jacket drove his high roofed van, that you could stand up in, up High Street. He always waltzed through the door with a box of crisps on his shoulder and a card of peanuts displayed on his forearm singing the line, And now for the latest fashion from Gay Paree – a hat with sleeves. Ha! Ha! Ha! And just when you'd be sitting into the tea, the burn lorry, heading with guts for Monery, left a smell the whole way up through the town that would put you out of it. The Captain always parked his car on High Street and he always had to be moving it.

One morning the bin men were waiting for The Captain to move the car so they could continue to nudge down High Street and collect the rubbish from the row of public houses. The tipper truck that they foisted the dustbins onto was ticking over. I was standing in the doorway and The Captain and Tom Flynn were in the car and ready for the off. On Low Street the girls in their royal blue uniforms were loading onto the bus for Carrick.

The car was an orange Maxi. I'd spent the previous evening in it listening to big eight-track cassettes of Johnny Cash. I'd been with The Captain when he brought it from Dickey's. Coming from the garage he had stopped in for one in Lowes on the corner and I watched the side door for him to emerge and when he did a shout in the street distracted him and I saw him wave, beckoning. I looked in the wing mirror and could see James Prior half running and half walking towards the car with his left hand pinning the flaps of his jacket to his stomach and a cigarette in his right hand. When he got to the car he put the cigarette between his teeth and opened the door and jumped in beside Gerard Molloy, my best friend, who was with us for the spin. The Captain got in at the same time and the car shook and the doors banged.

—Godbleshyamightyman, James said breathless. Did ya get a new yoke, Paddy?

—No, I have her just while the Wollesley is in with Dickey.

The Maxi had a front wheel drive and it could go up the Bakery hill in frost without batting an eyelid, Dickey said. But this was June, no sign of frost yet. Gerard Molloy asked would she hit the ton and The Captain put the boot down passing out by the grey concrete water tower that supplied the whole of Carrick, and I felt big because I was in the front.

—The maxi is like the tinkers ass, hard started but a whore to go, James Prior said, as we sped by the dump with white plastic bags and black crows flitting; by the house in the trees that moved when it rained and then passed the house with no door that Frank McGovern said The Captain had built, and laughed. A swirl of smoke rose from the cigarette between the fingers of The Captain's hand as it gripped the steering.

James pulled on a Woodbine. He was always looking for a lift but he knew all sorts of things about cars. And there was a smell of cigarettes and sweet whiskey-sweat and aftershave off him and it clung in the air and I couldn't make up my mind if it was nice or not.

It was James who said, If you put the yellow wrapper off the Lucozade bottle on the headlamps you'd see better in fog. That's why all the French yokes have yellow lamps on them coming out of the factory, if you ever looked, but you can do the same thing with your good butt of a lucozade wrapper.

—Fog and frost, The Captain said, and the sun cracking the stones. You'd think it was the middle of winter the way yourself and Dickey are going on. And The Captain told him about the front wheel drive and Prior said Dickey was right and started going on about an old Beetle the brother had that was hard be't and it would drive on top of six foot of snow. Like the time they were snowed-in above in the pit of a Christmas Eve and if it wasn't for the Beetle there'd have been no turkey. It was June!

And it was him suggested putting the tin foil inside the hubcaps to reflect the guard's radar, or wrap the number plate in cellophane so they can't get a photograph of the plate.

—It puts a sheen on it and the camera doesn't pick it up.

—But there's ne'er a camera round Ballinaglera. The Captain said.

—There might be the odd one up round Dublin.

—Well I'll not be going to Dublin in this.

—Or if you were in 'round London.

—I'll har'ly make London this week now, the way the thing has gone.

—Boys that would be on the continent would do it. If you were headin' down through France with a trailer-load of meat for Angola you might. And it was him suggested that you could jam the pop-up headlamps on Kilraine's new TR 7 with a tuppenny bit and when he'd head off at night they wouldn't come up and he'd be rightly fucked.

That was a new one. Molloy had told me about putting sugar in the petrol tank or sticking a spud in the exhaust. Things you could do at Halloween. Or wedging a milk bottle under the wheel and when they'd drive off they'd break the milk bottle and get a puncture. But you had to put the milk bottle on the rear passenger side so the driver wouldn't see it getting in. We'll try that one on the Head Master I thought.

We sped past the cross on the hill and across the hump-backed bridge in Leitrim and turned sharp right for the church and pulled into the pumps under the road for a pounds worth of petrol.

—Did Dickey think she'd run on fresh air, The Captain asked. The man's terrier barked for the pound note and took it in his mouth and ran off into the shop.

Anyway, that was coming back from Dickey's the day before. Now they were all set to go and the bin men were waiting. The Captain turned the key and there was just a click and nothing and he did it again, click and nothing, and again, click and nothing.

—Fuck Dickey anyway, him and his orange Maxi, The Captain said.

—That's like the battery, I heard Tom Flynn say.

I thought then that it might have been because I left the lights on when I was in the car listening to Johnny Cash, but I said nothing. At least not now and the state The Captain was in. First not finishing his breakfast on account of the rat and now this.

Then Tom Flynn got out to push with the ruler with the brass tips in his hand and The Captain stood on the street with the drivers door open and his hand on the wheel and we began to push and the bin men joined in shouting to The Captain, Sit into her Paddy, and, Try her in second. I pushed as well and felt big in between the bin men.

By the time we were at The Tailors she had chucked and bucked and started. The bin men cheered as The Captain revved her loudly at the bottom of the street beside Shanks TR7 waiting for Tom Flynn to catch up and jump in. One of them shouted, Keep her lit, Paddy.

7

TOM FLYNN'S CILL—THE RULER WITH THE BRASS TIPS—TAY—HALF A CHANCE

I called the cill nearest the sink Tom Flynn's cill because Tom Flynn would just wander in the back door when we'd be at the breakfast and sat on that cill like he owned the place. He sat on the cill with his back to the window in his blue bib overalls and tie and cap and jacket with his legs crossed, leaning his elbows on his knee with the mug of tea out in front of him laughing loudly—his grey hair curling out under his cap. He had a boxwood fold-out rule with brass tips and black painted numbers in the slim pocket on the leg of his overall, and he'd take it out and leave it on the table while he sat with his legs crossed having the cup of tea and laughing.

No, he'd have no boxty. All he wanted was a mouthful of tay in the bottom of the cup, he'd say.

—Wooh, that's plenty; lovely stuff; a drop of milk; just a half a spoon; just a taste; that's plenty; grand; loads; had a drop before I left the house. And the stirring spoon clinked off the side of the mug and then he'd shake it and rub it off the leg of his overall before leaving it back on the table.

My Mother and The Captain enjoyed him but he annoyed

me. Sitting there watching us having the breakfast. He'd sit there with his mug of tea and when my mother would tell me to eat up, he'd butt in and say, That'll put hair on your chest like bull wire, and then laugh his gravelly laugh. According to Tom Flynn everything puts hair on your chest like bullwire, no matter what you were eating—rashers, boxty, porridge, potato bread, black pudding. If my mother said eat up, he'd butt in. But I knew how I could annoy Tom Flynn. I'd scrape the painted numbers off his boxwood rule with a nail if I got half a chance.

8

HIGH STREET—FATHER DUIGNAN—JOHN ARMSTRONG'S ALSATIAN—ANNIE MAY —THE SACRED HEART LIGHT

Inside the window of Donnelly's Restaurant, in black, his white collar matching the white tablecloth and white napkins sat Father Duignan, eating his dinner from one to two every day. I always knew when it was two on the dot because Father Duignan came out the door of the restaurant, down the steps, his neck loose in the white collar, his newspaper in his hand, into his black Beetle with the chrome bumpers, and away. You could set your watch by him.

Father Duignan heard confession and I didn't like going because I had to make up lies about things I didn't do at all just to have something for him. Fr. Duignan only ever gave me one Our Father and five Hail Mary's. It was the same the time I'd found washers in the jars of nuts and screws that The Captain kept on the shelves in the middle shed and tried them in the slot machines in the Market Yard and they worked toppin'. Sometimes I'd only say three Hail Mary's because the church was an odd place to be when it was empty or because I was looking at the roof trusses and their big black iron brackets and their big bolts and wondering how they got them up there. But mostly I looked at the sacred heart light. The sacred heart light dangled, on a long chain from a high truss, high over the alter rail—it seemed impossible to get at and I wondered how they changed the bulb when it blew.

After dinner also, Deccy Moran the man who owned the bicycle shop behind the grocers and the pub and the undertakers on Convent Avenue came up the steps by the lime tree on his way back to the cool dark sheds in which he worked. He lived on the Carrick road and went for his dinner at one to two everyday and he always smoked and wore greasy jeans and glasses and a wooly jumper or was in his rolled-up shirt sleeves of a hot day. He walked fast and mounted the footpath at Kilraines and had to lean out to go round the precarious corner and to avoid the sandstone cill of the Red Bank that protruded to push him off the footpath. Himself and Johnny that worked with him knew everything there ever was to know about bikes. They said Raleigh was the only bike.

I bought my first bike off Deccy for a fiver. It was a done-up woman's bike - handlebars and rims were hand-painted grey. It wasn't a Raleigh. It was a bike he had put together out of bits of other bikes. It was a mongrel he said but she had steel rims and that was the most important part.

I taught myself to cycle. Round and round in circles in the back yard, afraid to stop. I tied a half a football boot lace loose on the front axle to keep it shining. Then I put yellow insulation tape on the spokes and noticed spots of rust coming through the grey paint on the rims.

Sometimes, if the likes of John Armstrong with his slicked hair and brown face, like he was back from abroad, was up and down the street with his Alsatian dog, I couldn't kick ball. Armstrong came down from Dublin in a black suit and white shirt and shiny new shoes. He always had new shiny shoes, but no tie—that was one of the things about him. Another thing was nobody ever seemed to know how long he'd be home for. Was it one week or two or maybe even three? Nobody seemed to know, and I often wondered if he knew himself. He'd wander the High Street with his big Alsatian dog early in the morning. Heavy steps. And might stop in front of Donnelly's and look down the length of the Carrick road to Mc Cormack's pumps wondering which pub he'd start in or would he head back up to the Big Smoke today. It didn't seem to matter. He came in and drank in the town all day and walked round with his Alsatian dog and I knew if I made a sudden move I was a gonner. It seemed he could stay as long as he liked. As long as it suited him. He had pucks of money, my mother said. Made money in England in the sixties. Where's there's muck there's money, The Captain said. But I wanted him to go because I couldn't move a muscle with that Alsatian dog watching me.

And daily, down High Street Annie May Mc Govern came walking quickly with flowers for the altar. She never said a haet. She sometimes rang the church bell as well. And sometimes she carried a light brush or a mack rolled tightly under her arm in dread of rain and there was always a good chance of that. And there was also a good chance she helped change the bulb in the sacred heart light. I thought Tom Mc Govern, that's Annie May's father, must have changed the sacred heart light, because he did everything 'round the church except say mass. Weights and Measures said, He'd have a go at that too if he was let.

Tom was a big burly man with a black donkey jacket and gangster hat and every day he passed my house at ten to twelve and ten to six and then the bell would ring. And ten minutes later he passed by in the other direction. Everyday. He was like clockwork. Sometimes he stopped and stood sideways in the door of Shank's and rested with his back to the jamb with one foot in and one foot out of the shop and talked into Shank who'd be chopping chops or mincing mince in his blood covered white coat.

Then the Nugent brothers would come down High Street on their way up to the convent after the dinner. One in his white shirt and tie and sleeves rolled up and the other with his jacket and waistcoat on him. I could never tell the difference. I just knew they helped the nuns with the garden. They were old and wore caps and always carried a bill hook or a hedging knife or a spade in winter or a scythe or a fork or a rake in the summer when they helped the nuns with the hay. I thought they might have something to do with changing the sacred heart light if it blew, though I was beginning to think it never blew. There was one in our drinking room and it never blew. I was beginning to think, Maybe that was the thing about sacred heart lights—they never blew.

9

THE BAKERY—STUFFING TURKEYS—BAY CITY ROLLERS—BURNT TO A CINDER

The bakery was a long low building that ran into the hill. On one end it had a low, wide red door and on the other windows that I could touch the top of. The inside of the bakery was dark and the lights were always on. The machine for slicing the bread stood directly inside the door. There was the machine for wrapping barmbracks and buns in clear cellophane and the stainless-steel oven with black knobs, for baking. And there was always the smell of fresh crusty bread that gave me an appetite for a thick slice of batch with soft butter and Bo-peep strawberry jam.

I knew the bakery because I brought the turkey up at Christmas to get it done in the oven. I stuffed it with bread crumbs and herbs and an onion and stitched him up with a darning needle with a big eye in it and black thread and put rashers on him and carried it the whole way up High Street on an aluminium tray. Pat Fanning cooked it and the giblets in the big stainless-steel oven with the black knobs. Pat cooked turkeys for half the town in that big oven. And at Halloween meself and Joey stole bracks out of the bakery and ran up to the back of the old school and hid behind the toilets, and opened them up to get the rings out. __

Joey was always wearing his brother's clothes. Tank-tops with orange scorch marks in them and brown boots with zips in the sides and he even had a pair of mottled red and black loafers with a woven pattern on the top. Larry Welch put quarter tips on the heels to make him sound like a horse and at night he'd come tearing it down the bakery hill on his bike and put the foot down and watched the sparks. And the toe was square shaped and I knew I didn't want to get a kick in the hole from them.

Joey's brother thought he was Nobby Clarke from the Bay City Rollers. And he hung around with the other big boys from the town who wore trousers with tartan stripes down the seam and shirts with tartan lapels and pocket-flaps and red monkey boots with big grips and yellow lacers and wrangler jackets like the skin-heads and boot boys that would smash your head on a gate or kick you in the balls or attack you with a bicycle chain. I knew things like that happened in other places, like Castlebar. And they were always talking about fights but there was nobody else in the town to fight with or playing soccer on the street with a burst plastic ball that was as hard as the hob of hell and welted from trying to fix the punctures with a hot poker.

Anyway, there was trouble the next day when the headmaster saw all the brack strewn at the back of the toilets and was going to find out who did it because people were starving in Cambodia and it was so bad he had the whole of the sixth class picking itchybacks to send out to them. Joey said he wouldn't eat an itchyback if you gave him a million. The headmaster said the brack-eaters had to be from the town and was looking at me when he said it. But I said nothing and knew he couldn't torture me like the Brits were at in the North. But then he asked Joey and Joey was annoyed because I had gotten the ring and he told the master that I had the ring in my pocket. I made a run for it but the Master grabbed me and pushed me into the corridor and bending over double stuck his big face and bony finger into my face and gave out about telling lies. I could see the chalk on his lapels and his pioneer pin up close, with the heart, and the cross bogged into the top of it. He made me write ten times I will not tell lies in future. I knew the Master tried to make the line as long as possible by adding on the 'in future' bit. Getting the lines made me cool because it was the most lines anybody had ever gotten in second class. But I was only cool until the following Tuesday, when Charlie Wynne held his mickey a secret way and made his piss hit the ceiling in the boy's toilet.

Because of where the bakery was located, the night it burned me and my mother watched out the upstairs bathroom window to our right and saw the sky blazing, and heard the crackle of timbers, and glass breaking and slates shattering. There wasn't a sinner asleep that night. The whole town was awake. Every last one of them. Even Mrs. Dowd and Mrs. Mc Kenna from the shop. They were both in our house at three in the morning. I'd never seen Mrs. Mc Kenna in her nightgown and without her glasses before. She was afraid our house would catch and go up and the children would be burnt, because it was thatched and it was in the middle of the town and then the whole town would go up along with it and then we'd all be burnt in our beds. Burnt to a cinder. A cinder!

—I'll take the poor craturs for the love of Jesus, she said, before they're burnt in their beds.

—With the help of God they'll be safe, said my mother,

and ran up the stairs to keep an eye for sparks out the bathroom window.

—Isn't one fire in the year enough for you? Mrs. Dowd shouted after her. My mother ignored the remark.

—Didn't that gossan of yours, meaning me, nearly fry the child in the cot, meaning my sister, and him smokin' above in the bed, for the love of Jesus.

—The boys from the Carrick brigade are above, my mother responded.

—The boys from the Carrick brigade are a cop bunch, replied Mrs. Dowd and stormed out.

10

T.J.'S—TOMMY AND PADRAIG AND EUGENE—DELIVERIES TO DRISTERNAN—GOING AND NOT COMING BACK

Sometimes my mother would send me over to T.J.'s for parsnips and I'd come back with turnips and sometimes she'd send me over for turnips and I'd come back with parsnips but she never got vexed.

It said, T.J. Mc Manus, over the door and everyone called it T.J.'s, but T.J. was dead this good while and his son ran it. And you could set your clock by him too. Every evening after the shop closed he'd leave through the hall-door, walk fast down Low Street, cross over at the Market Yard House, up the four steps onto High Street in front of The Tailors, then along by Shanks to the red bank on the corner to deposit the days takings in the night safe with the secret keyhole. If only I could get my hands on that key, I often thought.

The grocery shop was to the front and the bacon counter was to the back where Tommy Mc Morrow, in a white shop coat, wrestled with large tins of corned beef. After poking and prodding with the knife he'd shake the tin vigorously and turning it upside down he'd say, It's the vacuum, and puncture the bottom of the tin with a jag of a knife and out would slide a perfectly formed cuboid of corned beef. He'd wrap it loosely in greaseproof paper and place it on the red slicer. In smooth circular motions he'd cut slices onto another piece of greaseproof paper he held in his hand. He always said the jelly in the bottom of the tin was the sweetest. Then he'd wrap it in brown paper and pulling the cap off with his teeth he'd write the price on it with a marker from the breast pocket of his white shop coat.

If The Captain wanted anything like tap washers or a hank of window chord or a pound of three-inch ovals, two pound of two-inch wires, brass butt hinges, tee hinges, bolts, locks, a fuse, number twelve screws, blue tacks for nailing down carpet, he'd say, Go over to Padraig in Tom Joe's. And I always knew I'd find Padraig in his navy blue shop coat, in the hardware section. Padraig wrapped everything in brown paper. He had a big wide roll of it up on the counter that he could pull a length and tear it off all with the one hand. He'd lift a clump of two-inch wires clung to other from a timber box among a row of timber boxes at ground level and throw them into the brass bowl of the scales on the counter and put on a weight and get it balanced and pour them out onto a sheet of brown paper that he'd just torn off with the free hand and wrap it and write it in the book. And in the afternoon he'd do the deliveries in the Volkswagen pick up. A bottle of gas up to Joe Blessing in Dristernan, two bails of turf briquettes down to Mrs. Mc Partland in Carricknabrack. I was only in that blue pick-up once when Dick Flynn took me, with an earache, from The Feather Mc Keown's field in it. That was when they were building the football pitch.

If I wanted anything from the yard I'd still have to go to Padraig and he'd give me a docket. I'd bring the docket down the steps to Eugene with the tartan cap and red tassel on it in the yard. He'd be standing in a dark shed smoking and see you coming and then we'd go into the first shed with the low brown boarded ceiling and one light bulb hanging from a chord that I could touch if I wanted. I could get the smell of meal and paraffin and there were little trays of orange rat poison around the place. He'd take down a piece of wire with other dockets on it from a nail in the ceiling inside the door over the scales and stick my docket on it and hang it back up and then weigh out a half-stone of clarinda into a paper bag, for instance, and if I needed something upstairs like three gutter bolts and nuts and washers or a swan neck, he'd have to turn on the light and go up and get it. So when they were robbed I knew the window that was broken but nobody knew how much or what was taken. I was over for a fill of blue paraffin for the heater in the kitchen two days later and I was going to ask Eugene about it but Padraig said he had gone to England. I knew some lads went to England to earn enough to tax and insure the car and I knew some lads worked in the pit to get enough money to go and not come back. Everyone seemed to be disappearing. Going away forever and not coming back.

11

T.J. AND T.P.—LIZZY BUGGY'S—SWANLINBAR—MOULDY LOAVES

Bread men and vegetable men delivered to T.J's. The likes of Pat the Baker delivered batch loaves and T.P. Prior delivered vegetables out of his big orange truck that read, T.P. Prior, Fruit and Vegetable Importer and Distributor, Swanlinbar, Co. Cavan. I had watched T.P. Prior for years over the High Street wall with his cap and tie, make his deliveries to T.J.'s. Parked awkward on the corner he'd run with boxes of fruit stacked on his arms or four stone bags of spuds on his shoulder—the pipe always in his mouth. Sometimes he'd wear a shop coat and sometimes he wouldn't—he was like Dessie Price that way. And he was like Joe Gibbons in that he wore a hound's tooth jacket with patches on the elbows. And I always knew he was finished when he'd jump up into the cab and take the docket book from the dash and saunter back into T.J.'s. But it was the 'Importer' bit that got me. I'd never spoken to T.P. and I wondered, To what foreign lands had T.P. traipsed to bring us our fruit and veg. And where was Swanlinbar and how big was it anyway?

When the bakery burnt, they built a big shed across the entrance where we snuck in behind Foley's to rob apples. A truck brought the bread from Ballinrobe every night or in the early morning to be loaded into Volkswagen vans and distributed to the shops. During the summer they sent relief drivers from Mayo and they'd stay in our house and if it was Dan Murphy he'd bring me with him on the run and I'd be in the front of that van for the whole long day and I could carry nine sliced pans in a shot. I'd get in when he had T.J.'s done and then we'd head for Doyles of Drumcong—sliced pans, packets of buns, the odd brick or soda cake. I loved the smell of the bread van. Dan Murphy was short with short muscular arms and wore tight black tee-shirts and a black belt with a big buckle and smoked majors and didn't eat breakfast. The first day on the road Dan said, Swanlinbar was the farthest most point on our round before turning on our tail for Blacklion, Glan, Lizzy Buggy's in Dowra and home with quick stops at country shops en-route. I knew from Weights and Measures that the Northern Bank in Dowra was the richest bank west of the Shannon, and Shank said when he did the meat run round the Christmas the Dowras paid him in American dollars. We headed for Rantogue and Jackie Lee's. Skimming across the countryside in that blue van, chatting and laughing, glugging milk from the carton and eating buns for lunch. At McCaffrey's on the mountain Dan put the pen behind his ear, twelve sliced pans on his arm and went through the door back-ways pushing it open with his bum. The bell rang and he called for me to bring the docket book. Mrs. Mc Caffrey was outside the counter sweeping and he whizzed in by her, said hello, squeezed her right breast with his free hand and laughed, deposited the loaves, took a few mouldy ones, gave her a docket and back into the van and away. Then onto Augh-nasheelin and down into Ballinamore and as far as Swanlin-bar, two stops there, and then back across the mountain.

Twisty windy roads. Haycocks and turf reeks and grey TVOs. Slowing down and asking farmers on push-bikes for directions to Timbuktu. Back through Blacklion, Glan, Dowra, Ballinaglera and home. I'll admit I was disappointed I didn't meet T.P. on his own turf, but now I knew where he lived and Swanlinbar was no bigger nor better than Drumshanbo. I swore then I'd never go away and leave The Captain and my mother and the High Street and all the Drumshanbo's.

12

CHESTNUTS—UFO'S—CENTRIFUGAL FORCE AND THE O.K. CORRAL

On cold September evenings when the crows came home early, I lit the fire in the Drinking Room. I knew the crows coming home early was a sign of rain. Also, on September evenings I gathered chestnuts across from the red oxide tin hut where I got my hair cut. The large chestnut tree hung out over the road. I loved opening the chestnuts and was glad and disappointed all at the same time. Glad to see the smooth shiny brown nut but always disappointed that it wasn't bigger. The chestnuts had to be big and hard to win at conkers. There were all sorts of ideas as to how to make them hard. Soak them in vinegar; leave them in the hot press for a week; carry them around in your pocket for two weeks—but that all took too long. There was a hole in the side wall of the fire place so one Tuesday after school, I placed four of the biggest chestnuts I had in the hole and set the fire. I piled on the turf. I was going to have the hardest chestnuts in the whole school.

Over the fire place in the drinking room was a narrow mantle for leaving your cup of tea or pint on. In the evening The Captain sat around the fire talking about UFO's and centrifugal forces with Mick Woods, or the dentist, or Jack the Thatcher, or Con Ryan, or fitters down from Dublin to work on RB21's high on the mountain—fixing them when they broke in the wind and the rain—and drinking sweet tea and eating currant cake or treacle cake or apple tart or porter cake with butter. Bea, that came from Mayo to work in the bakery, before it was burnt, baked porter cakes and treacle cakes and huge apple tarts. It was in the Drinking Room drinking tea and eating porter cake with butter that The Captain hatched his big plan to set up the North-West Radio Controlled Aeroplane Club. He said, It never took off! Ha!ha!ha!

The Drinking Room was the room that joined the bar and the kitchen. It had speckled lino and a hatch for serving drink through. The joists were painted black and the doors a mustard yellow. A sacred heart light that never blew hung on one wall and a set of sharks teeth from Bermuda gaped down from a nail on the chimney breast. On the opposite wall hung a picture of me taken when I was seven. I'm on a pony at a late night fancy dress posing as Pat Taffe on Arkle. On my right, The Captain, in cowboy hat, dark glasses, and sheepskin coat. On my left, Shank Kilraine dressed up as a woman in high heels, eye shadow and fur stole. The Captain said, Shank is liable for anything. My mother said, Shank has a fine leg on him, and they're the right pair so they are—the cut of the two of them.

Beneath the picture of Shank and The Captain was an armchair and a table where Bernie Mc Keown sat on his own to drink quiet half-ones and where I got Jim Corbet to help me with my Irish. There was a bookshelf in the corner with blue hard-covered novels like Treasure Island and Robinson Crusoe and Gulliver's Travels but I never read any of them. Around the walls, box seats, that The Captain made and covered in bottle green leatherette, hid shoes, boots, spiders and clocks and there was a window in the corner that let light in.

If you wanted to get to the Good Room or go up stairs or out the front door from the kitchen you had to go through the Drinking room. My mother said it was like a train station. But I could sit there in my pyjamas watching the television and nar' a one would say a haet. The Drinking Room was where a country woman could wait and not be seen and then exit through the hall door with a baby power in her hand bag. The Drinking Room was where Mrs. Lynch of Derryhollow stood while waiting for the cure of the whooping cough for a sick grand-child. She was in every winter. My mother and The Captain both supped from a bottle of milk and said a prayer over it. And if the child didn't like milk they used a bottle of mineral, lemonade or orange or seven-up, it made no differ, it was the same thing and it worked just as well.

When Mrs. Gatts came in I couldn't look her straight in the face because I was behind her when the zip of her skirt burst going through Kielty's hall door to buy the Sunday paper. The papers were on a table in the hallway and the skirt fell cleanwork to the ground round her ankles. She never passed a bit remarks just pulled it up and asked Miss Kielty would she ever have a safety pin handy.

And if you were in to get take-out and cigarettes for a wake, or a station, or men at hay, you'd come in the front door and wait in the Drinking Room and then head off with yourself—quick and lively—your bottles in a brown paper bag, one hand clutching the bottom and two hundred cigarettes tucked under your arm.

The Drinking Room was where Weights and Measures hid out in the morning when he had heartburn and couldn't drink while my mother made him a concoction of bread soda and milk, or a shot of brandy and port to settle the stomach and make him right for the day. He'd look shuck. Even if the fire wasn't lit he'd sit by it with his legs crossed trying to spit woodbine flakes off the tip of his tongue and mumbling, It's not aisy. A few moments later he'd spit again and retort staring in the direction of the cold ashes, I suppose if it was aisy the women id be at it. If he was real bad he might just have a cup of tea and wouldn't talk at all. The Captain said he got kicked out of the seminary and was as sharp as a tack but was pure addled from the solid dint of drink.

The speckled lino of the drinking room floor was where The Captain gave wrashlin' lessons and showed me head-locks and Half Nelsons, the Boston Crab and how to implement a back breaking bear hug. And where big Ted Wallace if he arrived in par'lytic could take a fit of coughing from the cigarettes and creel over and you'd never get him lifted.

Through the hatch you could see down along the length of the bar to the Super Ser and slot machine down at the far end—the till, the optics, the salmon-pink timber shelves of glasses and bottles and pewter measures. I had to stack the shelves with bottles—all the labels turned facing out. Pushed in beneath the counter beside the beer cooler was a bottle bin for the empties and it was my job to tip it out the yard and sort the bottles—you have to know what bottle goes where. On the glass shelf over the till rested the bowl of a broken dudgeen with a harp on it that I found on the wall plate when we were taking the roof off the forge and beside it a florin, as my mother called it, with UFF stamped into it. Weights and Measures said someone with a chisel in a ship-yard got at it. A glass mug with a handle held money for bets and things that were lost. If something's found you'd keep it for a year and a day and if the owner doesn't show, she's yours.

The counter was high and a tiger orange colour that my mother varnished on Good Fridays. Three poor boxes were chained to it and I'd often try to get the money out of them with a knife—like the time I bought the Brooklax. Michael Gray had given me a square of that Brooklax on the street pretending it was dairy milk and then I went and bought a bar and gave a square to The Captain. That night, in the middle of the night sometime, I met The Captain on the landing—I was coming from the toilet and he was going to.

It was over the door or into the windows or under the seats with the spiders and the clocks that heads stuff copies of An Phoblacht that they never wanted in the first place. I'd find them and read them on a Sunday morning when I was cleaning up, Day nine, the war goes on.... But The Captain put an end to that after a bombing. He wouldn't allow them to be sold in his house and he told the head honcho from Ballinamore that too after we got a visit and us eating our dinner and The Captain wasn't even home from work, so they waited, two of them, in black top coats.

Even if we were having our dinner and someone came into the bar and wanted a mejum of stout you'd have to sit and talk to them about hay or skulling calves; but when my mother just left the two of them there standing at the far end of the counter warming themselves at the super ser and gave us out our dinner I knew something wasn't right. Then I heard the orange maxi pull up and the door open. I knew it was The Captain. I heard the voices and The Captain was having none of it. Then I heard the rattle of the bar door again and The Captain came in and sat into the table, lifted his knife and fork and said, Where's me dinner I'm famished, and my mother asked, Are the pair of bucks gone, and I watched him nod and take the plate and that's all there ever was about it more.

Anyway, that Tuesday evening, Jack the Thatcher and The Captain were sitting round the fire. I put on more turf and it was blazing. The Captain said to me, Go out you and hop on the kettle.

Jack wore a suit and tie even when he was on the roof and had a hat with a narrow brim that the wind wouldn't take. Jack had big hands and when he came down off the roof in the evenings he sat in at the fire rubbing tobacco and lighting his pipe and telling stories. Jack was from up at Tang, near the Three Jolly Pigeons, if you know where that is, and came to thatch the roof and I hoped that would put an end to the leaks. But I knew the crows would still be a problem and The Captain would have to keep the gun at the ready.

I helped Jack thatch. I sorted out the straw and tied it into bundles and brought it up to him. He showed me how to point scallops in three quick moves and gave me a knife and a sharpening stone to keep. Anyway, when the chestnuts exploded sending hard bits skidding across the speckled lino it put the hearts crossways in Jack and The Captain. The Captain said, It's like the O.K. Corral around here.

13

TIM SHANLEY AND HIS CURE FOR WARTS

One morning Tim Shanley, with his cart, was making his way down High Street. Tim's cart was made up of a metal frame on two bicycle wheels that carried two metal dustbins and when moving, his wide shovel and black bristled yard brush rested neatly on hooks along either side. As I approached he called me aside, into the gateway beside the house. I didn't know what he wanted and I was already late for school. It was the same thing with the barber. He gave me haircuts I never even asked for. I was beginning to wonder was it The Captain behind the scenes on the bush telegraph.

I knew Tim from being up and down the street every morning and I know he lived with his brother out the country somewhere. His brother was a cobbler with a short leg and learned cobbling by having to make his own boots. One with a high sole and heel to compensate for the short leg and now he was fixing shoes for other people. Tim wore a flat cap and long mack and his brother always wore a trilby and a light grey suit and tie and dark rimmed glasses, but he only came to town of a fair day. And even of a fair day the black boots would be polished and shone to the last and you wouldn't notice a thing. That must have been a thing about cobblers, they learned by making their own shoes, because Larry Welch was the same.

Anyway, I didn't know what Tim Shanley wanted but I followed him into the gateway and Tim took his flat cap off and placed it on the ground to kneel on and got down on one knee beside me and took my hand in his big farmers road-sweepers hand and looked at the finger with the wart up beside the nail. The wart was still white from the Compound 'W' I'd put on it. Compound 'W' was like acid, it was going to burn it off slowly. The Compound W came in a small bottle and I was on the second one but it was having no effect. I tried dipping it in the holy water font in the church porch every Sunday but that didn't work and there was a rock in the Fair green with a hole in it and water in the hole and I stuck my finger into that and said a few Hail Mary's and that was supposed to do the job but there was no sign of it ever to fall off.

Without saying a word Tim rummaged in his long coat pocket and produced two handkerchiefs, which he laid on the ground. And with his own wrist resting on his high knee he opened back the folds of the first one all the while holding my hand. On the handkerchief were five fresh green rushes laid out like spears, smooth and shiny, perfect—the very tips just beginning to go brown. He lifted the rushes one at a time and holding them at one end he proceeded to pull them across the wart like a fiddlers bow. He mumbled a prayer to himself while scratching the sign of the cross with a loose thumb on his own forehead, lips and chest and then replaced the rush gently back on the white linen.

He repeated the same drill with each rush. When that was complete he opened the second handkerchief to display five cigarette butts which he lined up in a row and proceeded to rub the sucked end on the wart in the sign of the cross, he did this more rapidly than with the rushes and with quicker shorter mumbles and when all was done he scratched again with the loose thumb, his forehead, lips and chest and paused for a moment, head bowed, before letting go my hand without saying a word. Then he rolled up his two handkerchiefs, stood up, slapped his cap off his thigh before placing it on his head and went back to sweeping the street.

I knew a lot about cures but I didn't know Tim Shanley had the cure for warts and I didn't know how Tim Shanley knew I had a wart and I never heard of the rushes and the cigarette butts one before. I wondered if he had the cure for warts in the stomach.

The wart was gone two weeks later.

14

LARRY WELCH—RAPID FIRE—BINGO—SONOFNEDMACS—HAIRCUTS

Larry Welch was a cobbler with a bad leg as well and nobody else I knew spoke as fast as Larry. I never knew what had happened but he built his house himself and raised his family with that bad leg; and he made his own shoes and he mended everyone else's shoes, and sold topcoats and car radios to farmers, and went to football matches and funerals and removals and bingo the length and breadth of the country, all with that bad leg. And he could shave the heads of countrymen sitting in his chair, with the electric trimmers. He'd shave the one side first—him, half standing half sitting with his butt propped on the bench—and then he'd move around, hobbling over shoes, dragging a loose trouser leg with a shoe attached to it and reposition himself propped on the crutch using the man's head for something to hold on to, before tackling the other side. And when it was done he'd send the countryman off saying, Tell them Larry Welch givesagoodhaircut givesagoodhaircut givesagoodhaircut.

After I witnessed what Larry did to the countrymen I never went to him for a hair cut. I'd go to Tom Mc Girl in the little red-oxide tin hut beside the bridge and under the big chestnut tree that hung out over the road. It had a small door and one window. Mr. Mc Girl would put me sitting on a stool a mile off the ground. The timber seat was shiny and arse-polished and I had to hold on to stay in it. For sitting quiet I got a lolli-pop that bits of clipped hair stuck to and annoyed me. But the countrymen were happy with their haircuts. And on Summer Sundays, content with the hay saved, they all sat on the left side of the church under the gallery with brown necks, washed and scrubbed and their Larry Welch haircuts.

Larry always sat at the bench, inside his window, surrounded by a sea of shoes, gluing or hammering, quick short taps—a leather apron covered in scabs of gone-off glue hung from his neck. Some people never collected their shoes and his shop was full of old shoes, but he knew where every shoe was and knew who owned every shoe.

—That woman nevercameback nevercameback nevercameback. He'd fire rapidly between taps of the hammer when you'd hold aloft a sandal in search of your own. Or he'd point with his crutch to a spot under a pile of shoes where a pair had lain buried for five years.

When I went down to Larry's and fought my way through the dark corridor stacked full of men's black suits and top coats he always greeted me the same way.

—Whoayoutaptap, Whoayoutaptap, Whoayoutaptap, he'd say moving the shoe around on the last.

—SonofNedMacstaptap, SonofNedMacstaptap, SonofNedMacstaptap, he'd say rapidly before I could answer, as he turned the last around on the leather apron. Itisn'ttruetaptap, itisn'ttruetaptap, itisn'ttruetaptap, I'd sing in my head, because Ned Mac had nar' a child and everyone knew it and I thought it was strange how Larry didn't seem to know it.

And he'd swivel the heel on the last tapping in tacks, taptap. The smallest nails you'd ever seen, taptap, lost between his black glue-smeared thumb and forefinger, taptap. He always seemed to hit his thumb several times before removing it and giving the final taptap and shouting, Topofthehousenine-ohtaptap, topofthehousenine-ohtaptap. Then he'd briskly wipe excess glue off his hand onto his leather apron and prod a switch on the wall with his crutch and start up the machine with the round brushes—the belt slapping and squealing and shuddering until it picked up speed and settled into a hum to smooth off the rough edges of the new heel and polish up the shoe. But he asked me that every time I went down to get a shoe mended, Whoayou whoayou whoayou, but he always knew which shoes were mine and I couldn't understand that. And Larry had the same haircut as he gave the farmers and I used to wonder about that too—who gave Larry his haircut?

15

FAIRY CAKES AND THE WALL OF DEATH—LIAM CLANCY—DOSED UP TO THE EYEBALLS—CUBBY HOLES AND GLORY HOLES—WHAT'S AN INCH?

It was on top of the chest of drawers that my mother cooled currant cakes or brown sodas or porter cake or apple tarts or rhubarb tarts that Bea baked. Bea Cullen came into our house every Tuesday and spent the morning baking with Dessie Price's cow's milk, Tom Joe Mac's flour, Mrs. Maguire's eggs, and Shane Mc Keown's rhubarb. And every evening at eight o clock, on the dot, The Captain would say, Run out you and stick on that kettle, and we'd have mugs of tea and currant bread or porter cake or a slice of rhubarb tart by the fire under the sacred heart light that never blew.

Mrs. Maguire or her husband or her son who'd had a good job in the bank but packed it in, would leave in the two dozen eggs every fortnight and they were left beside the bodhran on the piano in the Good Room and we drew out of them as needed. There was never a shortage of eggs round our house. Every fortnight, Mrs. Maguire or her husband or her son would leave in the brown leather bag with the eggs and head off round the town doing the shopping—over to Macs, into Crawford's, down to Daly's—and come back in an hour for the bag, the empty boxes and the money. That was the drill with the eggs. And Dessie Price who wore tangler's boots and rode the wall of death in England before he married would come into our kitchen, with big strides, and leave three bottles of milk on the table. He might be wearing a blue shop coat and he mightn't. That's what the fairy cakes that disappeared were made of, Mrs. Maguire's eggs, Tom Joe Mac's flour and Dessie Price's cow's milk.

The two dozen fairy cakes had been left on a wire rack on the chest of drawers upstairs on the landing the night the Clancy Brothers played the Mayflower. That big blue stout chest of drawers stood outside my bedroom door and as Weights and Measures would say, It's around since god was a boy—that and the safe with the old money. It was painted light blue the same as the boarded ceiling and it was minus two knobs. The drawers were full of trumpery and some of them stuck.

My mother should have known that leaving the buns on the chest of drawers on the landing was a bad idea and the whole town mad with the Clancy's in the Mayflower. They were en route to the women's toilet and anyone could get at them. I thought, any bad egg could come in off the street and tramp up the stairs and eat them.

But she blembt me straight away when she discovered the buns were gone.

—I'll brain ya, she said to me. She was like a briar.

I hadn't touched the buns but she wouldn't believe me. She said, she knew that I was the culprit, that I had devoured them and that she'd need roller skates to keep up with me.

—Who knows, I said, shrugging just to drive her mad entirely, it might have been the dog.

Darwin, our liver marked pointer, used to stretch out like a lord's bastard at the top of the stairs, catching the evening sun through the landing window before it dipped behind the corrugated roofs of the jam factory. But she said, she knew well it wasn't the dog and that she knew well the track of my hatchet—and that the dog didn't put the bun cases in the dustbin. It wasn't me but I knew who it was—it was Liam Clancy and Mick Woods who played the tin whistle through his nose.

I had heard the laughing and talking on the landing in the middle of the night and came out and there was Mick Woods and Liam Clancy with their ears back taking into the buns. It didn't surprise me one bit. No, that didn't surprise me. Nothing surprised me. One night in the middle of the night I was dead to the world, and my mother woke me to say hello to a black Bishop that was in drinking from Africa.

ANOTHER TIME too the Bishop of Darwin Australia was arriving and everything had to be a hundert. Cubby holes and glory holes were cleaned and scrubbed that hadn't been cleaned and scrubbed since his last visit. He came every four years to visit the Pope and dropped in en route dispensing rosary beads as he went. The house was full of rosary beads and koala bears that my uncle sent from Australia. The whole house was freshly painted inside and out. I loved the smell of the fresh paint. The press doors in the kitchen were newly glossed and all that was left was to screw the handles back on. Outside, the sheds were white-washed and the yard newly tarmacked. The place was immaculate. The Captain said, It's as neat as a robins nest. I had to run down to Campbell's for another packet of paste before closing. I knew The Captain had no time for the packet paste if he had his way, he'd just mix up a concoction of flour and water and it would do the job the finest. My mother was down after being up with Lilly getting her hair done. It was all go.

James Shannon was to the pin of his collar wallpapering the front bedroom off a beer crate for the Bishop. He just had to hang a couple of more strips but the hip was at him and he was dosed up to the eyeballs with disprin and brandy. He said it was the softy-faced buck of the Flynn's that pulled a chair out from under him at a wedding. I knew who he was talking about and I was laughing at the expression. Then he said he was a real haydog and it was a low act, the lowest of the low to pull a chair out from under a man and him just about to eat the dinner. I had mixed the paste in a basin and James let me cut round the light switch with a razor blade. I thought it was a good job and was pleased with myself, there was no gap. Well, none worth talking about anyway. But James made a thing about comming over and inspecting it and said, What's a quarter of an inch in a big country like Australia.

When he came the Bishop spent his time in the Good Room reading his Office and trying to arrange masses for himself to say, if Father Duignan would let him. That's why my mother said she didn't know what all the tarmacking was about, for not once out into that yard would he ever stir. She wanted the inside finished, and, she didn't care one whit if he never arrived. Bishop or no Bishop, all she wanted was the handles back on her press doors.

James was manoeuvring round the bed when I got back from Campbell's. He had the last strip cut and left folded and ready for pasting. When I had the paste mixed he hung it and slipped it to get it to line up perfectly with the half a yellow flower on the other strip and then brushed it in well. He worked his way down the wall brushing and rubbing hard and furiously as he went, from the middle to the sides, to make sure there were no bubbles. It was perfect. The Captain had a cure for the bubbles, he'd get a syringe off Doctor

Deasy and inject water into them and re stick them and you'd never know the difference. When James was below half way he got off the crate and let the last fold fall but it was about a foot short however he cut it. He stood back and looked at it and I chanced to say, What's a quarter of an inch in a big country like Australia, James.

He looked at me and winked and said, We'll push the bed in tight to the wall and he'll never see it.

16

FATTENING TURKEYS

In the yard a byre on the left housed a calf I had bought in Carrigallen mart for forty pound which I fed on Golden Maverick—the brand you could trust—and a handful of nuts that smelt like the malt from the big brown jar that The Captain spooned into us one winter. A byre on the right housed a pig, which I fed on porter slops and stale bread before I went to school. The Captain said, We'll fatten him up and kill him and eat everything bar the squeal and that's exactly what we did. And one hot day Leo Duignan and Pakie Mulvey malleted the pig and cut his throat and gutted him and hung him up-side down on a makeshift tri-pod in front of the turf shed and beside the Circus mans potato peeler with the green hose stuck down through his bum-hole flushing him out. Upstairs, in the loft over the turf shed I had hung a jute sack full of sawdust from a nail in the rafter for punching. I had gotten the heart in Shanks and needed the maggots for fishing. Further on another empty shed housed televisions and thievin' bullocks impounded by the sheriff. And sometimes our dog Darwin and another dog were locked in there to do the business. At least that's what The

Captain called it. I knew they'd get stuck together. The very top shed had been a cow byre when The Captain was a boy. The chains for tying up the cows were still on the walls and the trough for feeding them was still there with a channel in the middle for the dung. We never kept cows but we kept laying hens and geese in the top shed and I found eggs all over the place. Then, I found Darwin dead in the trough and I ran and told The Captain and he already knew and he said he was poisoned but only seemed annoyed that I interrupted him. I knew farmers put out poisoned meat to get the grey crows and foxes. The grey crows picked the eyes out of lambs. But how did Darwin get it if he lived in the town? He might have been off gallivanting with other dogs and I think he might have been hunting sheep because I'd heard other dogs in the town were and the Sergeant was out after them. Shooting them.

That must have been the first week of December just before the fair when Darwin died because The Captain was in the bar talking to Weights and Measures and Willie. They were talking about the Hoot Reilly who served in the fourteen-eighteen war, as The Captain called it, but who was long dead. I hadn't seen Willie for the whole of November. Willie went off the drink every November. Weights and Measures just switched from his usual rum and black to powers that he polluted with red lemonade and he said that was penance enough. Now they were in discussing Jim Sullivan and the price of turkeys. Weights and Measures said, Jim was out fodderin', found dead in the field. He just cut out. Willie said, It's a sight altogether, it can happen the best of us. And The Captain said, It's a holy terror. I knew then why The Captain wasn't that interested in talking about Darwin.

Jim Sullivan was the first person I knew that died. He came in of a Saturday night before mass for two pints and a half one to warm his stomach. He wore a black suit and v-neck jumper and white shirt and tie and a flat cap. His face was smooth and shiney as though from wear. He was another man that never sat. He stood at the counter, no, out from the counter, he never hung on the counter or put his elbows on the counter. He stood an arm's length away. Always stood.

He had been in the week before he died and he didn't seem great. He'd always ask for The Captain and my mother but that week he didn't. I started pulling the pint of Guinness and asked him how he was.

He didn't reply straight away just pulled his pipe from his pocket and scraped out the bowl of it with his silver penknife and tapped it on the leg of the barstool—black ash fell to the floor. Then he sucked on it and blew through it and I could hear the cold spit and tar from the previous smoke gurgle in the shaft and he banged it again on the palm of his hand and put it back into his jacket pocket. He then started peeling off shavings of tobacco, with the knife, off the edge of a dark brown block into this palm. Then he ground the shavings between the heels of his two rough hands and held the pinch of rubbed tobacco preciously in one hand and reached for the pipe from his jacket pocket again but with the pipe in his fist it wouldn't come from the pocket so easily and the coat lifted and he had to shake it off to get the pipe out and began filling it and pressing the tobacco down with his thumb. Then with the pipe clenched between his teeth he took matches from the other pocket and give the box a quick rattle before opening it and lit a match and held it upside down and let the flame creep up the match until about halfway and then placed the triangular flame across the bowl of the pipe and a quick flame rose from the fresh tobacco and he sucked on the pipe, long sucks, and his cheeks collapsed and the flame genuflected and prostrated itself and the tobacco glowed and he watched it with bright blue eyes, studiously, from under his cap. And when he was finished with the match but still concentrating on the glowing tobacco, he shook it vigorously at arm's length, like a nurse with a thermometer, and let it drop onto the floor. Then he used the matchbox like a damper on the bowl of the pipe to concentrate the draft. Closing and opening in rhythm to his sucking action. Matchbox up, damper open, inhale. Matchbox down, damper closed, exhale. Then short, quick, noisy, fishpuff sucks and smoke began to billow from one corner of his mouth and I could see his teeth and I knew she was nearly there and then he took the pipe from his mouth again and stared at the tobacco burning, and rearranged it, just the top layer, daintily, with the end of a match, and then with the pipe in his mouth he searched his two pockets simultaneously for the worn aluminium lid with the three holes in it and fit it snug onto the pipe. And then he plopped the pipe into the corner of his mouth between clenched teeth, and wiped his hands off each other and rearranged the pocket flaps and rubbed down the sides of his jacket with both hands and pulled contentedly a number of times and then answered my question.

—The thing's gotten horrid quiet, he said and pulled again on the pipe, hssss. It's just meself and herself out there now, hsss, just the two of us, looking into the fire, hssss, her in one corner, me in the other, hssss.

I knew Jim Sullivan had older sons who were all in America and now his youngest and the last of them had gone to join them and I wondered did Jim die of a broken heart.

. . .

I WALKED through the bar with an armful of turf for the drinking room fire.

—How old is turf, you that's going to school? Weights and Measures asked when he saw me, interrupting the discussion on turkeys.

—A billion and three quarters next May, I said, half to annoy him because I didn't know, but I knew he'd have an answer. He'd have the right answer or else it was a riddle but I couldn't let on not to know.

Willie had a pound of steak up on the counter and the blood was coming through the brown paper wrapping. He pulled deep on a Sweet Afton and blew smoke out through his loose gums and rummaged in the pocket of his rain Mac and pulled out an onion and left it on top of the steak. When Willie was drunk, he laughed and joked and sometimes fought with himself. Willie's wife was dead this good while and he cycled to town every Friday to get the pension and groceries and came into our house and always greeted me with sparkling eyes and a wink and two quick taps with his finger on his lips to remind me of our secret.

—Don't tell her or she'll not drink it so she'll not, he'd say. It was about the jaundice cure recipe that he had sworn me to secrecy not to disclose. I had seen the large lemonade bottle full of thick browny green glug that my mother was supposed to drink when she had the jaundice. Somebody up at Jamestown or somewhere had the cure for that. Willie had been asking for her and I told him about the bottle of glug. He said it every time he was in, drunk on mejums of stout and half ones, because he remembered how much I laughed the first time he told me what was in it.

—Ducks shit and gooses droppin's, he said, and I believed him, because that's what it looked like—thick browny green glug, and between deep drags on his Sweet Afton he swore me to secrecy.

—She'll not so she'll not. He said again and laughed into his mejum and shook as he laughed and the laugh became a cough.

I never knew if she drank it or not but she got better and Willie brought her in the biggest head of cabbage I'd ever seen that very week.

The Captain, Weights and Measures and Willie were discussing the turkeys. It wasn't exactly a discussion. Weights and Measures was quizzing Willie on the vagaries of the market and how to get the best price for a turkey and on how best to fatten a turkey. What would you give him? When would you start? And what would it cost? I thought Willie seemed reluctant to talk about the turkeys and he was more interested in talking to me about the jaundice cure. Finally, they all did their own calculations in completely different ways and came up with different answers but all agreed that there was no money to be made in turkeys.

The turkeys came to town squashed in like marsh mallows in a muckbox and covered with chicken wire. And Shank had severals hanging in his window upside down with unplucked necks and yellow beaks that dripped just one bead of blood and eyes that watched me. I was dreading Weights and Measures would ask me to do the sums on the turkeys. I knew his style so that's why I had busied myself with the fire in the drinking room but now I was curious about how old turf was.

—Answer me that, you that's going to school, he would say. As if he never went to school himself or could be excused for forgetting everything he ever learnt the day he left. He was on the rum and black and he always asked questions like the one about the hectares when he was on the rum and black. And he'd winch when he'd swallow and you'd see his blackened teeth and gums.

Weights and Measures wasn't his real name. His real name was John Boyle. I just called him Weights and Measures. How much oil could a gumboil boil, Boyle, he'd say and laugh when he was drunk. He always wore a suit and always drank rum and black. He never sat. Or if he was trying to catch me out he'd ask, If a fella met a fella in a field of beans could a fella tella fella what a fella means. How many f's in that You that's going to school? There's no f's in 'that'. Or if it took a week to wash an elephant what would it take to dry him? A towel. But his favourite was, What's smaller than a nat's knickers? A nits knackers. He loved that and laughed and delicately pinched a flake of tobacco off his tongue with his thumb and middle-finger.

One day he asked me, How many acres in a hectare? I got the answer and ever since that day he thought I had a brain in my head. But when he'd asked the question I just said I'd need time to think about it and went into the kitchen and got the red copy book from my school bag and all those things were on the back cover. How many centimetres in a foot and how many kilograms' in a tonne and how many hectares in an acre.

He had endless conversations with himself trying to work out the 'cubics' as he called them. How many cubic inches in a cubic foot and how many cubic feet in a cubic yard? I asked him once, how many cubic centimetres in a cubic metre and he was stumped but I had the answer memorised from the back of the copy. And then he asked, Did I know that land in Argentina was measured in leagues there was that much of it. If he was having a bad day he'd add as an aside, …and it's measured be the gallon in Leitrim, it's that wet. And, he said, I bet you don't know how many acres in a league, and he put a pound in a glass and we put it on a shelf beside the optics to be collected when I worked that one out. But that one wasn't on the back of the copybook. And another day he asked me did I know how many pennies in an old pound and did I know how many schillings in a guinea? And why was there a hen and chickens on the old penny? And did I know what a ploughman was?

Weights and Measures swirled the rum and black around in his glass and probed with the point of his tongue the cavernous recesses of his jowl as though in search of an angular eight of a peanut. Finishing off the rum in one gulp he grimaced and left the glass on the counter and said seriously, Turf is around since God was a boy.

Willie blew out grey smoke, and said to the glowing end of his cigarette, Herself used look after the turkeys. I thought then that that must have been why he didn't want to talk about the turkeys.

Darwin's body vanished and I never found out after where it went and The Captain never said a haet about it.

17

THE SCHKELPS MC GREAL

It was a thunderous evening in November, the crows were swirling above the high trees and settling in early for the night. I sat behind the bar on a high stool my feet barely touching the foot rail, listening to 'Hey Porter' on a four track cassette and making little chalices out of gold and silver cigarette paper to lick and stick on the ceiling and army tanks out of empty ten boxes. Through the large windows I could see the evening closing in. The lights were on behind the counter and I could see the indecisive street lights flicker on outside. The fire was lit.

I knew the drill if there was lightning. Turn off the television the radio and the lights, unplug everything, pull the curtains, stay away from the windows, don't answer the phone, cover all the mirrors with tea towels and make sure the milk was in the fridge

Mirrors were one of those things that always gave problems. If you broke a mirror you got seven years bad luck and if you looked in a mirror—at Halloween or during a power cut—with a torch held under your chin you would see the devil—so I didn't do that.

Through the lit up window I could see over the chicken-roaster out onto the street. Normally I would be able to see the bank door but a cattle truck on Low Street was blocking my view. I knew the truck had been there since the lunch when I ran down Bakery Hill and down High Street only to face a corned beef sandwich and pick up a packet of silver-mints in Donnelly's for Mrs. Flood.

The truck was a scrum of red and black bodies that looed and jostled and twisted and shifted from foot to foot, sticking their white heads and moist noses high in the air from time to time, and the whole truck would shake and creak and squeak.

From High Street I could look into the cattle truck and throw in bits of twigs and stones and land them onto the tops of their backs. Now, they still jostled and stuck their pink noses in the air and steam came from their mouths and wide-open nostrils. In the cold evening air steam rose from their backs like a low fog. As I watched the cattle jostle, a shadow appeared in the doorway.

The entrance comprised of a porch and two doors with glass panels in the top half. One door was fixed with two bolts, the other opened. I could see the shadow standing in front of the fixed door. Maybe it was someone waiting for a bus or a lift or pausing to consider the weather before going further. Then the handle squeaked and the door was pushed open but nobody entered. The shadow was still to be seen, not moving. I jumped from the stool and prepared to duck beneath the counter and run into the kitchen if it was someone I wasn't supposed to serve. Someone that was barred. That was the drill with that. Leave them and they'd just get bored and go away or sometimes they might give a few effs out of them or bang the counter before going out and leaving the door open behind them. They always did that, left the door open behind them.

I was peeking out between the Guinness and Smithwick taps and was ready to run when the shadow appeared real in the doorway and entered. I had never seen this man before. He was very drunk. He wore a khaki mac coat that you wouldn't see dried dung on and the tan elasticated boots, of a jobber. His hair was white and slicked back. He had a pointy nose and his eyes barely open. He came to the counter and stood beside it staring at some spot on the ground away from him, swaying, and after what seemed like an age rummaging for change he slapped down a handful of coppers on the counter. He asked and pointed wildly at the taps for a pint of stout. I started to fill it. He got the smell of chicken being roasted and wanted a chicken.

We roasted chickens on a stainless steel spit in the window that was blistering the paint on anything near it. They were set up in the window so people on the street would see it and get hungry and come in and buy a chicken. I could slide the chickens on the long bar three at a time, set the timer and get her going. It wasn't so easy getting them off because everything was hot and greasy but the smell of roasted chicken always made me starving. And I thought of a hot chicken sandwich with salt and brown sauce and the butter melting.

I slipped the chicken into a foil-lined bag with HOT CHICKEN written in red on it and a picture of a hot chicken on it. I used the bags to wrap my schoolbooks, turning the foil side out. I was the only one in the school with silver books.

When I had the pint and chicken up to him he pushed the coppers towards me with smoke stained fingers. I had to tell him it wasn't enough. He didn't have half enough for the pint never mind it and the chicken. I wasn't sure how he'd react. I put a brave face on it and said like a man, You'll need to go again boss.

—Fuck ya, he said, more is it, this town is getting dearer be the minute, Ye'll have me robbed.

Then I knew he wasn't from around and thought he'd lose it. But he put his hand in his pocket and pulled out a big roll of purple fifty pound notes I'd never seen one never mind a roll of them.

He stood flat on his feet, slightly swaying, trying to get the edge of the top note. He licked his dirty thumb and tried but it wouldn't come away. He must have licked that thumb five times but couldn't get the roll started. Then he banged it on the counter and said to me, Take one of them out of that will ya.

I peeled off a big purple fifty. It was huge. By the time I had counted him out the change he had the wad of notes back in his pocket and had the bag ripped open and was taking into the chicken there and then. He had come to life. He pulled and tore at the chicken and asked for salt with his mouth full. I ran into the kitchen to get it for him. He couldn't sprinkle the salt on it and asked me to do it.

—Aisy, aisy, he said, do you want to poison me. First ya try to rob me now you try to poison me.

He was now on a drumstick and pulling the skin off with his fingers. He gripped the flesh in his teeth and pulled his arm away with a jerk and took a nyomp out of it. Grease ran down his chin. I had the urge to wipe it with a tee-towel. It annoyed me so much I had to rub my own chin to ease the irritation. He gripped his pint with a greasy hand and I could see more closely the smoke stained fingers, dark brown around the nails. When he was finished he stood with his arms on the counter around the heap of bones on the foil bag and his head dipped until his nose almost touched the carcass and then it would jerk back up. He mumbled and tried to sing along to 'Ring of Fire'. This went on for about fifteen minutes until he stood out from the counter again, flat on his feet concentrating and swaying and rummaging in his mack coat pocket for his cigarettes and then in the other pocket for the matches. Then he swayed, holding his mouth open awaiting the cigarette as his body went one direction and his hand went the other. After the third attempt he got the cigarette in but was not able to strike the match so he plopped the matches and cigarette up on the counter and asked me to light it.

Smoking was nothing new to me. I had done it loads of times. I'd even tried the pipe. The cigarette was a Sweet-Afton and I could taste the chicken off it where he'd sucked and when I gave it back to him he said, Daycent schkin, daycent schkin and I felt grown up.

When he had taken a pull from the fag he tilted forward and started walking towards the door and out.

Having dumped the chicken carcass in the dustbin I was listening to 'A Boy Named Sue' and sitting looking out at the cattle truck when it started up. The cattle looed louder, and jostled each other in anticipation of the move. The truck revved loudly and put out a burst of black diesel smoke and jerked into motion. The lights were on in the bank and I could just see the tops of heads moving around.

A few weeks later he was in again. He was taller than I'd remembered and had bright blue eyes. He was all business and ordered drinks for the men with him. I could see in the day light his white slicked hair had a yellow tinge to it, but he was fresh and clean-shaven and had a white shirt and tie and jacket. He still wore the tan elasticated jobbers boots, the ones with no lacers.

I was afraid I'd call him The Schkelps to his face since I'd heard he hated it. That was bothering me. What if I said, How's a going Schkelps, by accident and so I said nothing letting on I didn't know him and thinking he wouldn't remember me. When he saw me he stretched his big paw in across the counter and said, Daycent schkin.

18

MRS. WYNNE—JAMES CAGNEY AND AL CAPONE—THE SUN JUMPING IN THE SKY—SILVER SPANNERS

It was Christmas Eve. The place was bright and the fire blazing when I left my mother sticking up fairy lights with cellotape and thumb tacks. The Captain needed me. He said there had been a hard frost the night before and every pipe in the town was burst and I had to help him fix them. We headed off, him carrying two silver spanners and a silver hacksaw all together in one hand. But I was reluctant. The Captain was always taking me places and delaying me, and Willie Wonka's Chocolate factory was on the television at half three. He'd say, Ah, come on now with me you for the spin, but he'd never say where he was going or how long he'd be. We could be gone the whole day and just when I'd think we were heading for home he'd pull into some house I'd never seen before and sit there drinking tea and talking for far too long. Or he'd pull up across from Joe Lowes on the corner and jump out saying he had to see a man about a dog. But there was no dog and I knew he'd be in with Joe Lowe, or Mrs. Lowe, chattin' and laughin' and drinking half ones and then he'd come back out and jump into the car and we'd be away again at top speed—headed for home, Mum and the dinner. And Christmas was even worse, he had to call into every house that ever had a light on, as my mother would say and there was always tea and cake and a quick one to help him stay between the ditches.

Our first call had been to the bank. The bank was a three-storey building and one of a block of three that lined Low Street. A large Christmas tree that you could see from the street sparkled in one of the upper windows. The bank-door was blue. It had a brass knob and a brass knocker and two bell buttons side by side with big brass surrounds that looked down on me like owls eyes. Inside it had a high mahogany counter and brass foot rail and timber and glass dividers and little glass doors with little brass bolts and little brass knobs. In the bank everything seemed right and like it had been there forever. The Captain had told me the burst pipe was in the vault and he needed me to help him before all the money got wet but we didn't see any money. It was straight up to the attic and he gave me a torch and a piece of string and said, Tie up that ballcock and give me a shout when your ready, the tank is below at the far end.

I put the string in my pocket and dodging the black cobwebs that hung from the rafters I followed with my hand a dusty purlin and treaded carefully on the ceiling joist, like he'd shown me. I'd never been in an attic that big before and I wondered how The Captain knew where the tank was and for a while I was thinking maybe there was no tank at all. Then, down behind the chimney I found the grey galvanised tank all on it's little ol' lonesome in that dark attic and it's brass fittings lit up like they were glad to see me under the beam of light.

—All right, I shouted back to where I could see the rays of

the landing light coming up through the hatch and I heard the ladder rattle and as he came into the attic he blocked out all the light.

—Shine that yoke over here, he said, til I see what I'm at, and he groped for a timber and pulled himself up the rest of the way.

—Where are you, he said, as he tried to look around the light beam. Shine it at me feet, he said, not realising I was dazzling him on purpose. Then I blocked out the beam with my hand and before he could swear I had it back on again.

—How did you get in there? He asked.

—Here, I said, using the light as a guide and showing a small triangular passage between three timbers.

—Only a snipes fart like you would squeeze through that, he said, and I could hear him puffing as he stooped and squeezed and came out of the dark from behind the chimney with the two silver spanners and silver hacksaw gripped tight and shining in the light.

—I was a bit thinner when I put this tank in, he said.

—Like when you married Mum, I said. I was thinking of the photograph of him and Mum and the Bishop of Darwin Australia on their wedding day above the mantel piece.

—That's right son, like when I married your Mother, and then he said more to himself than to me, And that's not today nor yesterday.

—And you had more hair too, I said, shining the light on his scalp.

—Less of your guff and shine that yoke over here, he said, I can't see a styme. He proceeded to cut the copper pipe where it had burst and rummaged for a brass fitting in his jacket pocket and in no time the pipe was fixed and he said, Let her rip. I pulled the one end of the slip knot that he'd shown me how to make and the pipes gurgled and the water splashed until it became a solid gulping sound as the tank filled and we left the attic.

—Is that it, I said, knowing it must be near time for Willy Wonka's Chocolate Factory, and dreading his reply.

—Just one more heist kid, he said, from the side of his mouth like James Cagney to try and win me over, and started telling me about a heist himself and Al Capone once pulled.

—Where too now, so, I said. At least he didn't seem to be stopping for tea with the bank manager and Mrs. Murphy.

—The Barracks, he said, the Sergeant and herself are flooded out above. This cold spell is playing puck.

I was interested in going to the Barracks but I didn't let on. These were better than some of his other jobs he'd have me on. But I was afraid because of the black hole. I'd never been to the Barracks before but I knew there was a black hole in it where they threw bold children so I was glad when we approached the private entrance. As we passed the Barrack door proper I stood on the outside of The Captain and stayed in step with him in case it opened but I glanced and I saw the chrome letter box that someone said the Sergeant peeped out through to keep an eye on the town.

The Sergeant opened the door on the private entrance and he was the full of the frame, his white hair almost touching the top of it. He had a big nose and he stood there with the sleeves of his blue shirt rolled up, his collar open and a ball of wet newspapers in one hand. I knew when I saw him that he was another victim of a burst pipe. I'd never seen him without his tunic or cap except when he referee'd the boxing in Doherty's hall in a white shirt and dickie-bow and I knew he could handle himself and he wasn't afraid of the Arigna bucks or the Aughnasheelins or the Black Provos marching up and down with their black flags waving. Weights and Measures said, that the Drumshanbo's were that tough, it was the only spot in Ireland that required a Sergeant of the Guards to ref a boxing match. I felt proud when he'd said it.

Keeping his free hand on the latch the Sergeant stood back to let us in by him.

—The hard men, he said, ye made it, and I felt important and checked my pocket to make sure I had the piece of string and we repeated the same procedure as in the bank. When we were finished the Sergeant's wife wanted to give us whiskey and I was delighted The Captain refused, which wasn't like him but my heart sank when he said he had to make another call. I knew now we'd never be back in time for Willie Wonka.

The lights were flickering on in the town as we made our way to Mrs. Wynne's. There was no light to be seen in her house and no light on the bell. The chrome letterbox was dull and corroding and the little rectangular knocker broken. The Captain could never just knock like a normal person but rapped out a loud tattoo on the glass and almost immediately I could see a light when a door opened at the far end of the hall. The hallway was cold and she led us along to the kitchen without putting on the light. The kitchen was heated by a small cream paraffin heater like the one we had at home for getting dressed in front of in the mornings. It was our third call but there was no evidence of a flood and I knew her pipes weren't frozen either because she filled the kettle from the tap.

Now, the last place I wanted to be was in Mrs. Wynne's kitchen but The Captain didn't seem in a hurry.He sat in the armchair by the cold stove, his coat and hat still on him, a cup of Nescafe instant coffee in his hand and puffing away.

He tipped ash onto the saucer until Mrs. Wynne jumped up and got an ash-tray. She sat back down directly across from him in what looked like her chair at the table. It had arms and a cushion unlike the other chairs and the newspaper she had been reading was open on the table. I was at the other end eating a thick arrowroot and drinking milk out of politeness. The Captain hadn't offered her a cigarette but she said she'd have one just to be sociable. I didn't think she was any good at smoking. She held the cigarette with the tips of her fingers and just sort of kissed at the end of it. She held the ashtray in her other hand with the cigarette lingering over it and any time The Captain needed it she'd hold it out and he'd reach across.

Mrs. Wynne wore her hair pulled back from her forehead and tied in a ponytail with a red elastic band. She had wide ocean blue eyes and eyelashes that reminded me of needles. I couldn't look her straight in the face. She thought I was shy. I thought, Mrs. Wynne's got needles sticking in her eyes. She was talking about God and Christmas and how she saw the sun jump in the sky in Mejogorje.

—What do you make of that, Paddy, she said.

—Sur I suppose anything is possible, he replied, a suitably vague answer that got him out of a spot. But she wasn't happy with his answer and she turned her bright eyes on me.

—What do you make of that Conor, the sun dancin' in the sky and all that.

—God can do anything he wants, I answered, while reading the writing on the biscuit. And she seemed much more impressed with that answer than with the Captain's.

—That's right, she exclaimed and jumped up to get me another arrowroot from the tin in the cupboard and moving around in a flurry she asked The Captain if he wanted another coffee and when she settled back on her chair she asked him directly, But isn't the boy right Paddy. Sur can't God do anything he wants.

—I supppose, The Captain said, reaching over to tip his ash.

—Those cigarettes will be the death of you, she said. How many do you smoke?

—Too many, too many, he replied.

—Won't they kill him, Conor? Do you want more milk? I wanted to get away so I said I was full.

—You should give them up Paddy, look at the money you'd save, and they'll kill you. My Martin gave them up two years before he died and he didn't know himself. He used to have a terrible cough but that all went. Do you cough in the morning Paddy? The Captain shuffled on the stool and before he could answer she turned to me.

—Does he cough in the morning, Conor?

—A bit, I said.

—In the bathroom, she asked. I nodded.

—You should tell him to give them up or they'll be the death of him. I'm fecked anyway, she said, Your father didn't smoke when I knew him first.

The Captain stubbed out his cigarette on the saucer and leaned over to leave it on the table and used it as an excuse to get to his feet and finishing off his coffee said, That was lovely Breege. That sounded funny because I'd never heard anyone ever call her anything except Mrs. Wynne before.

She stood in the door until The Captain closed the gate and I looked back and saw the light go out and the house darken. As we walked away I asked him did she not have a burst pipe and he just answered, No. But didn't she ring I persisted.

—She did, she did. It was just a Christmas call, son. And then half to himself, he said, The aul' Christmas gets horrid lonely. I knew then not to ask more. Then I felt guilty for wanting to watch Willie Wonka's Chocolate Factory and not taking more milk off Mrs. Wynne, just to be sociable.

On the way home I practiced carrying the two silver spanners and silver hacksaw all together in one hand.

19

GEOGRAPHY—THE MASTER AND THE PERFECT CIRCLE—TWENTY LINES

There was a good chance I was the only person in the whole school with Tippex. I got it off of Con Ryan—he said they used it in the bank the whole time. Con was a boarder in our house who worked in the bank and had the leaving cert and helped me with my Irish homework. I'd tell the master my mother or father helped me but he didn't believe it. I never told him it was Con Ryan from Lanesboro, thirty miles away, that helped me.

Now, geography, that was another problem I had. The Master would have us standing round the board in a half circle up at the top of the class. It was the board off to the side, not the main black board, a smaller one. One that he could draw a map of Belgium on out of his head and put in all the towns like Ghent and Bruge and Brussels, and ports like Ostend and rivers like the Meuse and mountains like the Ardennes, low-lying, all out of his head and leave it there for weeks until we were finished with Belgium and I thought it was a lovely picture even if he drove me mad with the questions and I'd miss it and feel every bit of it disappear under the duster, gone forever, like Eugene with the tassle on his cap. And then as he'd draw Germany on the board all out of his head and all freehand and then I'd miss that when he'd rub it out—forever.

And he could draw a perfect circle as well, freehand. There was a big compass in the press that you could put chalk into for drawing circles on the board but the master didn't need that. No, he had his own knack, like Georgie Porgie and the barrels. He'd stand with his back to the board with the chalk in his right hand touching the board behind at his hip, and with his left hand pinning his jacket to his stomach he'd give one quick twist of his whole body, like a half somersault but without his feet ever leaving the ground and without the chalk ever leaving the board and with his hair and the tail of his jacket flying he'd finish up facing the board and with the most perfect circle drawn. Then pulling down the tail of his jacket and straightening his tie and wiping a hand across his scalp to realign renegade hair he'd quickly pivot so he was facing the class again, standing, scanning as if he had never moved. He couldn't take his eyes off us for a second, so he couldn't. I don't know how he did it bar he was double jointed and could touch his elbow with his thumb but he drew the most perfect circle and he used all sorts of colours of chalk I'd never seen before. I thought he was the only teacher that was allowed use the coloured chalk because he was the Master.

He used red for cities, blue for the rivers and lakes, brown for the mountains, and he'd mark in forests with green upside down 'v's. He even had purple and yellow. And then he'd ask us all questions. He'd fly around his arm fully extended clicking his fingers and pointing his long boney finger; click click quick quick; Name that mountain range; click click quick quick; Gannon! Ardennes, Sir. Name that river; click click quick quick; Mc Partland! Meuse, Sir. Name that city; click click quick quick; McWeeney! Brussels, Sir. What do they produce in Brussels; click click quick quick and then he was pointing at me and I couldn't think and everything stopped the clicking and the quicking and everybody was looking at me and I couldn't think and he thought he was helping me and he said, You had it in your tea this morning and then I knew it wasn't Brussel sprouts but I still couldn't think and he went clicking and quicking until someone else got it and I got another twenty lines—I will learn my geography in future; because the answer was sugar and I never forgot that because I don't take sugar in my tea. I gave it up for lent the same time I did mass in the convent with the nuns every morning. I thought doing the lent was a good thing but it got me the twenty lines.

That was unfair and it annoyed me a bit but not too much because I had lines done already that he'd corrected for questions I couldn't answer on England and what do they produce in Sheffield click, click quick quick and they were the same lines, I will do my geography in future, I will do my geography in future, I will do my geography in future twenty times and so I just made his long red-biro ticks and his autograph disappear with the tippex and he never spotted it when I handed them up to him the next day.

I told Con Ryan what I did and he never said a haet and just smiled and I wondered if he used the Tippex to fool his own boss sometimes.

20

MITCHELL

Mitchell was blemt for everything. Someone even said he burnt the bakery but I knew that was wrong and wasn't fair. He hadn't even come to the town then. I knew it wasn't right to say things like that about someone if it wasn't true. But he had come back from England and was fit for anything. He had the knack for opening beer bottles and it was him had the idea to rob The Tailor's store.

Our back yard stretched the whole way up to the school football pitch and the boys clubhouse and the five big trees that stood tall and dominating. In them, crows built and refurbished their nests with a racket in the spring and cawed contentedly as they returned early from their excursions on November evenings. In the shadow of the trees was the high wall that surrounded the garden of the convent where the nuns grew vegetables. I knew that if I was caught on that wall or climbing the trees to look over that wall the nuns would take me in and put a skirt on me. So I didn't climb the wall. I also knew that you didn't drink egg water or pump air into your stomach with a bicycle pump. Both of those things gave you warts in your stomach.

I was sitting with Mitchell and Joey on the high bank under the Nun's wall and resting against the high trees. I could see our kitchen window and back door and watched for my mother in case she came out. My mother didn't like me hanging round with Mitchell. I was also keeping an eye on the gate that went out between the boys and girls toilets of the school for Father Duignan. That was the route he'd take if he knew we were hanging about the field. He hated us kicking ball in the football pitch after school or hanging round the boy's clubhouse and he patrolled the place like John Armstrong's alsatian. I knew Mitchell wasn't afraid of Father Duignan and was liable to say anything in his English accent. At Halloween he hid behind a tree so she wouldn't see him and shouted at Mrs. Doran that she was a bear of a woman. But Mrs. Doran knew it was him because of his English accent and she was waiting to get him. He wanted to put a banger in her letter box. From where we sat beneath the high trees I could see directly into The Tailor's back yard and could see the stores where he kept the drink.

Joey lived in the ESB houses on the other side of the clubhouse and he knew everything there ever was to know about sex but had never done it. He was an expert cee-bee'er and was always bursting to talk to lads faraway. He had a biscuit tin full of D-X cards that he'd got from cee-beeer's all over the world. The farthest I could get with my aerial was the Road Runner in Geevagh. Joey was also an expert fisherman. He preferred Shakespeare reels to Daiwa reels. I had one good Daiwa reel that I kept greased with vaseline and two others for bits and parts. One time meself and Joey hung a sheep's-heart from a rafter in the loft over the turf shed and it dripped maggots into a biscuit tin. We'd gotten the heart off Shank and we needed the maggots for fishing. Joey ett cornflakes at night time and reckoned we'd all get hair like

Mitchell's, but I had my doubts. Joey's older sister taught Irish dancing on Saturday mornings in the club-house, and gave out Crunchies to the girls. Joey and me hung round outside shouting like yobbo's and knocking on the windows and looking in and hoping she'd give us a crunchie or even half a one between the two of us just to get rid of us. I'd go to the clubhouse for training. The boy's clubhouse was where boxing training, press-ups and pull-ups and sit-ups, took place. It was also where the cubs and scouts met and the lower half stored burnt pots and camping equipment with bits missing. At the top of the hall beneath the stage there was a heavy bag and a speedball suspended between floor and ceiling with a stretched bicycle tube. There were gloves for sparring and mitts for the bags, all kept in a tea chest. I loved the smell of leather and the press-ups, and the sit-ups and the sparring and the heat that came off the storage heaters with the big stone in them. I had a poster of Muhammad Ali over my bed and one time The Captain stayed up with me in the middle of the night just to watch him fight. I wanted to fight in Doherty's hall where the big tournaments were held. I could eat a raw egg in milk for breakfast.

Doherty's hall was always full of noise and sweat and Sweet Afton smoke. Doherty's Hall was all black eyes, burst lips, sweet tea and swollen noses and Manorhamilton boys and tough bucks from Kiltyclougher that talked funny and triangular mountains of triangular sandwiches of blue band margarine and ham and jam sponge cake in chunks that would choke a horse and Mrs. Dowd from the shop and Mrs. Ferguson who was stuck in everything, and Mrs. Doyle, the Sergeant's wife, with her hair in a bun pouring out tea with milk in it from big pots with two handles into enough cups for an army and big bucks, bachelors with blackheads, digging into the sandwiches in the side room and me and Joey squeezing between men in black topcoats with stuffed gobs, and laughing to steal a second slice of jam sponge cake. And the Sergeant was always the ref in his white shirt and dickie bow.

But at Halloween there was a problem with the club-house. The light was going on and off by itself. I didn't like the sound of it. I had just come to terms with the Boogey Man, Jack Frost and Wee Willie Winkle—all three looking in my window at night. Faces outside the window, always there, ready to pounce. When Mitchell got wind of the ghost he wanted to go on a stake-out and wanted me to go with him but I wouldn't. I think that's what we had the fight about, yon time. I got him in a head-lock like The Captain showed me on the drinking room floor and was telling him to submit like Mick Mc Manus or Giant Haystack or Big Daddy would do on the BBC, in black and white, at four on a Saturday. After that I thought to myself, Mitchell wasn't so bad. He's left me alone since.

Mitchell used the edge of a stone in the Nun's wall to prise the cap off the Guinness bottle. He positioned the crimped rim of the cap on the stone and hit down on it with the heel of his hand. A spew of white foam came out and he had to hit it again before the cap was free. He took a slug and said he hated Guinness like he was an expert. Then he took another slug. But Guinness was all I could get. I took the two bottles from the first crate inside The Tailor's store door and legged it. I wasn't going poking round for two pint bottles of Harp for Mitchell. I didn't like the taste of the Guinness and handed the bottle to Joey. Mitchell opened the second one and slugged from it then he opened his trousers and showed us this mat of hair, he'd been going on about. I thought he must have got an injection to make it grow like that because he was the only one of us that had any. I didn't know what to do and was in dread my mother might be looking through the kitchen window at Mitchell and him with his trousers open.

As the bottle went around it reminded me of the under twelve final when the Mars bar kid played in goal and afterwards we passed the cup around and there were bits of tayto from other fellas mouths floating around in the lemonade but I didn't care and drank from it anyway. At least with a Guinness bottle you couldn't get bits of tayto into it. But I knew Mitchell was liable to spit in it on purpose just so's he'd have it all to himself.

Mitchell didn't play football or box but he knew how to make a bomb. You just put a piece of carbide that we got from the miners coming home from the pit in a jam jar and added water and put the lid back on and ran. And I showed him how to make a peg gun with elastic bands and the metal spring from the middle of a clothes peg as the bullet. It would cut the eye out of your head, so it would. I fired it at bottles and crows but Mitchell took it off me and hit Tim Guihen, who wouldn't say boo to a goose, on the forehead and left him with a lump that came up like a duck egg. Guihen had a sister who won three golds and two silvers at the swimming in Mosney and now she was after Mitchell as well.

But, anyway, The Tailor must have spotted me taking the two bottles and before we had them finished my mother was calling to me from the back door and I knew by the sound of her she was going to throw the book at me. I thought I could tell her we were eating rhubarb like I used to do with Mc P when I was younger. Coming from school I'd throw the schoolbag in our door and go straight down to his house and eat his dinner and then we'd spend the whole afternoon in his garden with the sugar bowl eating rhubarb and digging holes to Australia. Ah, they were the best days. But then there'd be a fight about the homework when I got home.

My mother was like a briar. She said she'd knock lumps off me and knock the street out of me with thumps. She was at the end of her tether, she said. She said she heard about the Guinness on the bush telegraph and I couldn't deny it because I knew it was wrong to tell a lie. There was a whole litany of things she said. Complaints from the bank manager about the tunnel meself and Molloy dug, and complaints from Ann next door about the C.B., and now The Tailor. She said that I'd be going away to school and that would put a halt to my gallop. That was the first I heard about that and I knew she was annoyed but I didn't think she'd send me away. I thought she was just saying it because she was vexed. And I wondered did The Captain know about it. I was waiting for her to bring up again about the time I locked Paddy Flanagan in a wardrobe in one of the rooms in his father's hotel and couldn't remember which one. And Paddy's father, Paddy senior, had half the town searched before I told him. That was before Paddy Flanagan left. He had been my best friend and I missed him but I knew this was different. I shouldn't have robbed the bottles and I don't know why I did it. Mitchell wouldn't do it because he had done it before and The Tailor said he'd castrate him if he caught him at it again.

The thing with Ann next door was this. The Captain had bought me a C.B. and I had it set up on the filing cabinet inside the kitchen window. My name on the C.B. was the Red Baron, the debonair German fighting ace and I could speak to good buddies in Keadue and Arigna and to the White Lady over round Boyle. Everyone wanted to talk to her. Anyway, for weeks on Friday and Saturday nights Ann had charged up and down High Street to see if anyone was in a car talking on a C.B. because it was coming out over the speakers in her singing lounge. Camillus and Ricky could be in the middle of, lets say, Coward of the County for instance, and my voice would cut in over the music. Breaker, breaker for a copy. When Ann discovered I was the culprit she'd raid through the back door but I'd be gone. I'd break off conversation with the Firebox or the Hotdog or Chubby Checker when I'd see her shadow flit past the window and only return when the coast was clear to sit earwigging on the White Lady for the rest of the evening. Earwigging, that's what you called it when you were eavesdropping on someone else's conversation.

And the thing with the bank manager was all Molloy's fault. Molloy lived in the bank and read Warlord and made model airplanes with UHU glue and used the sheds at the back of the bank as his HQ. The sheds were dark and had no escape route. Every HQ has to have an escape route, he said, so he suggested we dig a tunnel out. That whole winter we dug and dug. Every day after school we dug down through the black daub to get under the dividing stone wall and into the next shed. Down forever. It had to be big enough for a quick exit but the evenings were getting short and we abandoned the job but not before having dug a knee-deep hole in the dark shed.

Mihaul Mc Keown swept out the porch and shone the two owl's eyes with brasso every day after he opened the bank's door at ten. He polished the counter inside in circular motions with Mr. Sheen and the windows outside in figures of eight with windolene. Mihaul kept the place gleaming until he went down to the dark shed looking for something, probably the spade, and fell into the hole and broke his wrist and that put a stop to his circular motions and figures of eight. Me and Molloy had to lie low for a while and decided to build a morse code transmitter upstairs in my house. I got the instructions for the transmitter from an encyclopedia that was on the shelf in the drinking room and I commandeered a whole roll of grey flex belonging to The Captain from the middle shed and got two flash-light batteries, that you could put your tongue on to test, in T.J.'s. I rolled it out upstairs—from the front bedroom across the landing down the narrow passage with the low ceiling to the back extension and into the back bedroom with the windows that went to the floor. If you were put in that room and got out the wrong side of the bed you could put your leg through the window. That's what happened Jim Sayers once, he was that drunk. He ripped his leg up the back and there was blood everywhere, on the sheets and on the carpet and he had to get stitches in the middle of the night. Anyway, that aside, I ran the cable behind wardrobes, under beds and underneath the carpet. At the back bedroom I cut a chase for the flex through the door-saddle with the breadknife so's the door would close. Then I set up my transmitting and receiving units attached to the two batteries. I was in the back bedroom ready to transmit and Molloy was in the front room ready to receive, but nothing ever happened. I couldn't understand it. I just left the grey flex running round the house. My mother never mentioned the grey flex, I don't think she ever spotted it.

Anyway, the next day my mother wouldn't let me out of her sight and I had to stay in the yard and couldn't go beyond the gate up into the garden that brought you up to the Nun's wall. She put me sorting the empty bottles saying the devil made work for idle hands.

With the empty bottles and the smell of sweet sticky beer there was always wasps and blue bottles round our house and when I had finished the bottles I followed them to see where they were coming from. I tracked one wasp to the turf shed. I found the hole in the turf stack where the wasps were going in. I stuffed it with paper and lit it. The paper burned but seemed to quench and only annoyed the wasps, so I left it. But it must have took and there's still a black stain on the whitewashed wall where flames rose and were licking the ceiling joist when The Captain discovered it. The Captain said after, Only for I spotted it the whole place would have gone up. But he was bamboozled. He couldn't understand how it happened. I knew he was vexed though, because he didn't tell me the one about the time himself and Red Adair fought brush fires out abroad in the Congo. I was afraid if my mother found out about it I'd definitely be sent away to school, so when The Captain interrogated me about how the fire might have started I just said, Mitchell done it.

21

THAT SORT OF AN EVENING— MINERS—A HALF ONE AND WATER—IF THE HANDBRAKE EVER WENT

The sun was dipping behind the corrugated roofs of the jam factory. The ten to six bus from Sligo had dropped off a roll of evening newspapers and an engine part, with a brown cardboard tag tied to it. Tom Joe's son was closing out the shop doors and Gerald Early pulled down his blinds. Gerald Early was a gentleman. He told me once that he woke up in the middle of the night and found a mouse sleeping on the pillow beside his ear and he picked him up and walked down the three flights of stairs in his pyjamas from his flat over the men's outfitters and let him out the front door onto Low Street.

Cars for Ballinaglera and Arigna had gone through and it was that quiet time before the dinner when the sound of the ball echoed and I waited and waited for The Captain and Tom Flynn to return. My mother had placed a chair on the footpath to catch the last rays of the sun as it lit up the front of the house and penetrated deep into the bar. I watched Mihaul go home with his wavy flaxen hair parted and combed to one side and his blue shirt the colour of the summer sky. He had the neck of his shirt open and the sleeves rolled back from his wrists. His navy blue v-neck sweater hung through the hoop that his arm with its hand in his pocket made, it was that sort of an evening. I was lying on the white line in the middle of Low Street looking up at the pale blue sky and waiting for cars.

The road was warm, and I could smell the tar and down that close you could see small bubbles of tar that swole and burst. I looked up at Molloy's window. He'd be having the tea. He had his dinner during the day, with his father the bank manager. Bank managers and their families could have the dinner during the day. I followed the telephone wires from pole to pole and thought of September and when the swallows would line up to leave, and the swifts would leave. Headed for Africa and I wouldn't see them for another year. And I followed a single wire from the pole that ran right over head to a fitting under the thatch. Swifts swooped from the eaves of the thatch, and I watched as they soared and bickered and soared until they almost disappeared and then plummeted and swooped again. And then Bernie Kane was standing over me and shouting. He looked huge and it was hard to recognise him looking up from my position on the road. Bernie wore a hat and ox-blood jobbers boots with elasticated sides and a long jobbers mack coat that you wouldn't see dried dung on and cycled a bike and brought us in carrots. He was in the fire brigade and when the siren would go off you'd see him come flying around the Carrick Road corner on his big black mans bike and head up Hill Road to the fire station. Shouting and pulling me by the t-shirt he pulled me up the steps by the copper beech and in the hall door to my mother and gave out to her for letting me do it—lie on the road. And going out, shouted something about if I was his son, and how I was lucky I wasn't. My mother said, That aul' effer, and I don't know if she meant it or not but she ran me up the stairs with the wooden spoon saying she was going to knock the flittin' and gaddin' off me. It was the only time ever I missed dinner and it was Bernie Kane's fault.

That evening I had to content myself with looking out the hole in the broken window as I waited for The Captain and Tom Flynn to return in the orange maxi. When The Captain did finally arrive back himself and Tom Flynn were half et with midges and they had to have a glass of beer each, they were that thirsty. The Captain had brought back a set of pram wheels for the go-cart I was going to make and had a ball of white putty in greaseproof paper he wanted me to soften. The putty was like mawla but had dried out and I had to add linseed oil to it and soften it up. It was a job I'd done before. It was a ball the size of a mans fist and I kept at it, pressing it and rolling it and folding it and flattening it out and rolling it up again, like a lump of dough until it was smooth and moist and had no hard bits. It was a man's job and I loved making thumbprints in the putty and smelling the linseed oil off my fingers.

As the sun slipped away, it's warm yellow light lit up High Street and the front of my house and threw crisp rays across the bar floor and up the counter and across the counter top and jumped to glitter off the chrome of the optics and the mirrors behind. Standing in the doorway and blocking some of those rays was Mick Woods looking at the jam factory and thinking of dancehalls in their hay-day or the music scene in Manchester or Birmingham. He stood in the doorway, with a flute case in his hand waiting for his brother and a Smithwicks. He always waited in our house for his brother and always drank Smithwicks when he waited in summer, and stout when he waited in winter if he wasn't doing November. And in winter he stood in the Drinking Room under the set of sharks teeth that hung from a nail on the chimney breast, with his back to the fire and his black flute case left on the mantel piece. He wore a light grey top coat, he was the only man I knew with a light grey one. And if the brother was late, trouble with a cow calving maybe, or a bullock stuck in a gripe, he'd have to have another one and might open his coat. And the brother would arrive in a station wagon loaded to the hilt with speakers and microphones and drums and they'd head off to wherever they were playing. And Mick played the flute and could play the tin whistle through his nose.

I knew Mick, who was standing in our doorway waiting for a lift, could see to his right down to Jimmy's door and could see, standing in the shade, Larry Welch who in his black suit and gangster hat waited on his timber crutches for a lift to a removal or bingo. Topathehousenineoh.

He stood in the doorway of Jimmy's making small talk with Jimmy and farmers who had the hay saved—happy farmers with shiny red faces and hayseed in the turn-ups of their trousers and in the cracked creases of their boots, in to buy the Observer or a pound of ham and a few tomatoes. And to his left Mick could also see Paddy Mc Cormack, hackney man, at the Carrick Road corner, waiting, half a leg gone. The missing half itched for weeks after, but he didn't give up, he got an automatic when no one had an automatic, that he could drive with one leg and continued as per usual, waiting propped with his back to the wall resting on his metal crutches. Waiting to bring someone home in his automatic hackney or bring someone to a removal or to bingo. Topathehousenineoh. And I knew Larry who needed a lift could see Paddy who wanted to give him a lift and Paddy could see Larry. But no one moved.

. . .

TOM KANE, brother of Bernie's, in cap, suit and hobnailed boots, crossed High street in three long strides from the top of the steps by the lime tree and in the hall door of Shell House for a pint after he had parked the lorry at the jam factory. No doubt, to talk with Frank Shanley about his run to Tuam or the docks in Dublin, with a load of jam on.

Frank who was dark and coal dusty, tied his horse to a telephone pole on Low Street. A big tired, lumbering horse, with big square leather blinkers stitched all round, after bringing a load of coal down from the top of Arigna mountain—straining to hold her on Church Hill—eating from a nose bag while Frank drank whiskey and swopped livery stories with Tom, in Shell House. That's the way it was sometimes even on November nights when there'd be a fog down and halos round the street lights and chimneys putting up smoke and not a car to be seen, Frank Shanley's heavy horse would be tied to the telephone pole on Low Street.

PADDY REYNOLDS on his last run of the day from the pit drove up Mill Hill and pulled to a halt in the middle of the square, in front of Jimmy's and in front of Shank's, and across from Kielty's where his metal sided tipper truck discharged its cargo – miners. Miners with black caps, black clothes, black faces with white eyes peeking and black lunch bags strapped across their shoulders carrying black sandwiches to be eaten with black hands and white teeth. One by one they jumped off the back of the truck and got onto Honda fifties or into cars or went into Kielty's, or McMorrow's, or into Missus Mc Kenna for a paper or a cone or silvermints or into Shank's for a steak, and up to Tom Joe's for the onions to bring home. And Paddy, a tidy, short, square, pipe smoking, tight bit of a man in suit and boots dulled from coal dust, calm and consistent, drove off and parked in his usual spot across from his house just at the top of Hilly Road facing the town and walk down and go into Mulveys for a half one and water or two. I could see the lorry from The High Street. It was always there, the very same spot, teetering on the top of the hill it seemed, just planked there, turned and ready for the off in the morning. And I wondered what would happen if the handbrake ever went.

THE SIREN WENT OFF. The sound hung in the air. I watched the Carrick road corner for Bernie Kane and hoped he had gotten the whole way home before having to cycle the whole way back in again. Sure enough he came around the corner. Usually the tails of his jobber's mack would be flying but he was in his shirt sleeves and hat and humped over the handle bars pushing the bike on. As I waited in anticipation for the brigade, I imagined the flurry of activity. Pulling on boots, hats, cumbersome coats half on. A car sped up Low Street probably another fireman leaving a meadow of hay or the dinner. And then I heard the engine slowing at the turn for Carrick and the revving and the front of her rising as she passed Paddy Mc Cormack. He raised a hand off the crutch handle and waved. Blue light flashing, no siren, just the high revving roar of the engine and I watched as it turned down Mill Hill heading for Arigna. A bog fire high on the mountain, maybe. Larry Welch waved.

22

SCHOOL WAS ON THE HORIZON—NAR' A CHANCE OF A REPRIEVE—SEWING TAGS ONTO UNDERPANTS

I thought I should have failed the exam and there wouldn't have been one haet anyone could have done about it. But I passed. I had made my own bed. I had seen the school, with its tall windows and high ceilings and hard floors and toilets that echoed, and I didn't like it. It was big, and its football fields were big and the class rooms were big and the grounds were fenced and closed off with a big iron gate. I dreamt of that big building with its hundred tall dark empty windows, like black eyes on an empty ship bobbing away out in the middle of the ocean, with me in it.

The day I told Weights and Measures I'd be sent away was the day he told me he'd spent a while studying for the priests in the Irish College in Louvain. And he said he could speak Walloon but I didn't believe him. I just thought it was another word like Timbuktu or Baluba and that he was making it up. And I thought about how the master with his Antwerps and Bruges never mentioned Louvain. Weights and Measures said it was where he had learned to drink and smoke and a smarter man than he would have stayed at home. He had a bit of French as well, he said. I couldn't believe he had been anywhere. He hadn't the set about him of someone who'd been anywhere. The collar and cuffs of his jacket were greasy and the cuffs beginning to fray. You could see a black rim on the collar of his white shirt. He never seemed to change his clothes except for to put on a v-neck jumper under his jacket in winter and it only came off if there was a persistent spell of good weather in July or August with the sun cracking the stones and bubbling the tar on the roads.

—Nar' a chance of a reprieve so I suppose, Weights and Measures said, looking glum.

—No, I said.

Shortly after the lying on the road incident my Mother started sewing tags onto collars of jumpers and shirts and waists of trousers and backs of underpants. And she had a pile of clothes as high as the chimney below on Arigna power station, up on the chest of drawers on the landing and it kept getting higher. There was a letter with a crest on it—a broken wheel. And all the items were listed out; runners, togs, football boots. I was going to be away for years. I'd burn the lot if I got the chance, I thought.

I began to think they just wanted rid of me. Maybe it was the gallivanting on the High Street, or the robbing of the apples, or the drinking of the stout, or the smoking, or haranguing Maureen Mulvey when she was trying to teach the girls and Mickey Saunders Irish dancing.

After the incident with The Tailor she always had something for me to do. Manage the premises, as she'd say, go down to Campbell's or over to Tom Joe's, or down to Larry Welch. So she was sending me away to the penitentiary and there'd be no more fighting over the homework. They'd put manners on me. I thought I'd run away to my great uncle the King Mc Manus, the King of San Francisco. Then I thought

I'd be able to wangle my way round The Captain. Me and him could pull plant and ride out west, and he could tell me all the stories he wanted about Al Capone and Davey Crockette and John Wayne and the Alamo but when I asked him he just said it was probably all for the best. And I knew by him he didn't want to say more. Now, the only man in my corner, my second, my Angelo Dundee, was Weights and Measures. There was still hope. I knew he'd talk to The Captain.

As the time got closer I did more of the jobs round the house but there seemed to be no softening. I started getting up early and cleaning out the fire place. And setting the fire if need be. I washed all the glasses and swept the bar floor and pulled the curtains and got ready to open the doors at half ten. The Captain was usually gone and I'd clean away his mug. If he got up on his own he'd just put a spoon of tea leaves into the cup and have a cut of Bea's brown soda and jam and away. My problem was I couldn't even roll a barrel, not to mind tap one.

George worked in Donnelly's stacking shelves, sorting bottles, rolling in full barrels, tapping barrels, rolling out empty ones, sweeping up floors, wiping down tables, mopping out toilets, emptying ash trays, giving them a wipe, polishing mirrors, cleaning out the ashes, setting the fire. I didn't know if George worked behind the bar but surely he was well able to pull a pint, let it settle and put a head on it. There was a knack to that. You had to hold the glass sideways under the tap and let the stout roll down the side of the glass, not splash into the bottom of it because you'd have bubbles on the top and the auld bucks would be giving out yards about the bubbles on the top. I was just learning but even the most easy going man would be telling you how to do it and get narky if there were bubbles on the top or if there was too much head or too little head. The smart ones would say, You could put a half one in that. Meaning that the head was too big and there wasn't enough stout in it and that you could top it up with a whiskey.

Georgie Porgie, that's what I called him, was old and small and wore a suit jacket that he kept the silvermints in, but he had a good knack for rolling barrels and one day he showed me. At least that's what he called it, the knack. George's hands were calloused and rough from all the work and he would give me a dry-shave if he got near me. But I was getting used to George and would just ask for a silver mint but stand well back. The dry-shave as George called it was when he got me by the lock and pulled upward rubbing his rough finger hard across my temple. But the knack to rolling the barrel was being able to steer it with your foot. It was simple when you knew how. If you wanted the barrel to go straight ahead you pushed it in the middle but if you wanted it to go right you pushed on the left hand side and if you wanted it to go left you pushed it on the right. All with your foot, and with your hands in your pockets and sucking on a silvermint. That's what I learned off George.

By late August the pile of clothes on the chest of drawers was getting higher and higher and then finally a brand new bag appeared and it was left stood beside the chest of drawers. It was a big brown leather bag with a strap and zips and pockets at each end that zipped up. And then new pyjamas and a wash bag arrived. This was getting serious. The pyjamas were one thing but I had never seen a wash bag before. I had a tooth brush only one other time when I went away to Boyle with the scouts for a weekend. That was before I got the boot but that's a whole other story. I'll tell you about it some other day. In Boyle, meself, Mc P, Murph and the Mars Bar Kid were in a two man tent. The Mars Bar Kid was in charge because he was the eldest. We were crushed in like turkeys in a muckbox at the Christmas fair, and the rain drummed on the tent for the whole weekend. It was so wet you wouldn't stick your nib out and I woke up with my arm sore and Murph told me it was from the Mars Bar Kid trying to give me a chinese burn after I fell asleep

This was over in the Forest Park in Boyle, now, and I had a new tooth brush for the trip and pink toothpaste that tasted like bubble-gum. And we washed and spat out at a tap screwed onto a tree in the rain. That was the last time I had washed my teeth. I didn't know what toothpaste she had bought this time and I wasn't asking. I didn't ask anything that might make going away real. I just watched as the pile grew higher and the suitcase appeared. I thought, if I don't ask any questions or say anything about it, itjust might go away. I woke up every morning and came out to the landing hoping it might have vanished. I just thought it might all disappear and there wouldn't be another word more about it and I could just stay there and look after the bar, wiping out ashtrays and sorting the bottles, rolling in kegs. I could get my own breakfast as well and I wouldn't have to bother my mother for that either.

Then one day Weights and Measures came in and it must have been a long good spell because I remember he had his jumper off and he gave me a ten pound note he took rolled up tight out of the inside jacket pocket like he had it kept aside especially. At first I thought it was a bet that he wanted me to hold and I went to put it in the glass on the shelf between the optics but he told me to hold onto it meself.

—Stick that in your pocket, he said, that's for going away. I didn't believe him. My heart sank. He was the only other person I knew that thought it was a bad idea and now he'd turned turk on me as well. I didn't know what to say.

—Throw me up a rum and black, willya, he said, and

intently counted out change on the counter. I put the rum and black up to him. He took a gulp and dragged from his cigarette. He was quiet for a while, then he said, Sur it might be all for the besht, and delicately picked a shard of tobacco off his lower lip. Prince was dead, Darwin was dead, I knew I was alone. I haven't seen Weights and Measures since.

23

THE HORIZON—ORANGE STREET LIGHTS—MAYO AND GALWAY—BEA AND HER TARTS

Now, the brown bag is pushed under the bed with a tag with my name on it in case I get lost like an engine part sent up from Sligo on the bus. Everyone else is asleep. Lying here I look up at the high ceiling. I can't sleep and don't think I will. There are no curtains on the tall windows, just one half of a timber shutter. Through the other half, the orange street light comes in as it pleases.

I've never seen an orange street light before. The light throws the squares of the window across beds that other lads are asleep in and down on the floor. It's not like the orange of the sun that streams into our kitchen and lights my mothers face in the morning or the orange of the sun that brightens up the front wall of our house before it dips behind the jam factory in the evening. I know there'll be no crows laughing their heads off in the morning delighted to be awake, and no Captain to come in singing and lift my mother off her stool and waltz her round the kitchen. No more glorious mornings. I might have to go to the toilet in the middle of the night but I don't want to. It's too far away and down the loud stairwell. I don't know what time it is now or how long I've been lying here thinking about Drumshanbo and every one and every thing in it, down to the frogs in the well, but a buck came round earlier and turned off the lights and then he came round again and told us all to shut up and he wasn't one bit nice about it either.

There's lads from all over Mayo and Galway. There's a lad in the bed across from me. He's the only one whose name I know. He's a Sean Tuohy from Craughwell. That's a funny name...I wonder could Craughwell be anything like Drumshanbo. Hardly. And I'm thinking again about how the sun rises above the tops of the tall trees that the crows nest in and how it creeps slowly down the bank wall and by ten o' clock the whole street has brightened up. I know it will do it tomorrow and I wish I could kick ball in the bright empty street. But that won't happen. I'm stuck here. And I can feel the water works beginning to start. But why did I have to leave that house. The house was me and I it. I knew every nook and cranny in that house. I knew where the clocks, the spiders and mice lived. I caught thirteen mice in one week emerging from a hole behind the armchair in the kitchen. I knew the house upside down and inside out and I didn't want to leave it. It was my whole life. I thought again about meself and Molloy taking turns pushing each other up and down the High Street on my sister's tricycle. We were too big but I'd sit on it and he'd push and then jump onto the back at top speed holding onto my shoulders, and I can feel his grip still, and we'd whizz past The Tailors and down by Hocks. We took turns doing that until it broke. Who knows but I might never see Molloy again.

And there'd be no more go-kart. I made a go kart from the pram wheels that The Captain found in a ditch somewhere. With a plank and a timber beer crate with the front knocked out for a seat. There'd be no more Georgie or Paddy

Donnelly, or T.J.'s son in his white shop coat, no more Weights and Measures, no more Tim Shanley and his warts, up and down high street pushing his cart, sweep sweep. And no more Tom Flynn to persecute me and tell me boxty would put hair on my chest like bull-wire. And I think that my heart will burst and that I love all these men so much. And the tears are beginning to roll down my face. I'll have to be quiet, or the other lads will hear me. I think about Larry Welch and I loved him and his shoes and boots and black top coats and Deccy and Johnny and their done-up bikes and Mrs. Dowd and Mrs. Mc Kenna and Bea and her tarts and curney cake and the Sergeant and his wife with her hair in a bun, and Tom Mc Govern and his bell ringing and Annie and her flowers for the alter. I loved the High Street and Low Street and the Drinking Room and the clocks and the spiders and all the mice I had killed and I was sorry for that now. I think of my mother. I know she likes jazz, John Wayne and Seven Brides for Seven brothers. She likes the word synchronised and hates the word ojus. She likes Turkish delight and Fruit and Nut and hates latchicoes, haverals, black Provos and rats. She drinks tea from a china cup and likes to put the milk in first and reminds us that she was named after the Queen. She has two books on the shelf, both of equal size and both in brown paper covers. One is the dictionary and the other is a cookery book. She goes to Dublin for the day on the train and gets her hair done with Peter Marks. She dresses us in the morning in front of the parafin heater. She loves Ceili House and Sunday Miscellany, and sits in the gallery at nine o clock mass and we sit with her looking out over the altar and the sacred heart light and Fr. Duignan, and down on the men's side, down on burnt heads and Larry Welch hair cuts. My mother doesn't come from Drumshanbo. No. She comes from Arigna, along the Arigna river valley. Daughter of Long

John, neighbour of Pat of the River and Tim Dinny with his shirt hanging out and one time she said I was the cut of him. The Captain said she was an Arigna, or one of the Arignas. He'd say it like you'd say someone was an Apache, or an Arapaho, or from some other tribe that took scalps. Even though Arigna was in Roscommon it wasn't far away. Just head out the Galley, cross the Shannon, put the shoe down and up the railroad. That's where she comes from but she loves the sun and I think, she thinks, she's a daisy. If the sun was cracking the stones she'd sit in the sun amid the beer crates and the glaring white washed walls on a deck chair with her eyes closed and her face skyward keeping an ear for the rattle of the bar door. Every so often, she'd move the chair following the sun. Like a daisy my mother opens up in the morning by pulling back the long curtains on the kitchen windows to let in God's daylight. As the sun streams in and warms the whole place and lights up her face, she says, It's going to be another scorcher when that haze lifts.

And I imagine The Captain doing his usual before going to bed. Sticking his head out the front door to see if anyone or anything is moving. The light in Jimmy's that lit the square would be gone and other lights dim as the town turns in. In Shank's butchers the violet light from the fly zapper casts an eerie hue over the idle contents of the shop—the display cabinet, the worn butchers block, the band saw, the till. The stainless steel hanging rails glint blue. He crosses the dry concrete to the brown cut-stone wall to a place beside the copper-beech tree and like a captain at the prow, leans on his thumbs and knuckles and looks onto Low Street. He looks straight ahead to the bank, no light. He looks to the right, down to Jimmy's shop and to the left up to the Barrack door. He looks into the darkness of the run-down sheds in the Market Yard to see if there is anyone running guns or wrecking the phone box. He leans on the wall and enjoys the quiet of the town and waves at a lone car that toots as it whizzes past. I wonder does he think of me as he watches the feeble wisps of smoke from a dying fire, goaded with a smooth-handled poker into a last hoorah, rise up into the darkness above the town lights. In the morning he'll get up and shave first thing and cough cigarette coughs. Blow out his cheeks, pull the razor across and pump air into his lower lip. He delicately cuts under his nose. Ploshes water up on his face. Blows out noisily. Around the back of the neck. Splashes. Big Blow. Rinses the sink. Down he'll go, shoes in hand, thinking about making phone calls. Ringing hardware's and roofers in Sligo and Mohill. Pressing five penny pieces, one after the other, into the metal box in the hall way. He'll open the front door and go out onto the shaded street to see if anyone or anything is moving. He'll cross the dry concrete to the brown cut-stone wall that runs the length of High Street to a place beside the copper-beech and leave his shoes on the wall rest on his thumbs and knuckles and watch for ice-bergs. He'll see Mr. and Mrs. Steady, slicked and curled, come walking on the footpath around the Carrick road corner—past T.J.'s closed shop-door and pass along in the shadow of the bank heading up to mass in the convent. T.J's son, exits his hall door and follows them not far behind. Cars from the Ballinaglera direction accelerate as they come up low street and take the turn for Carrick on two wheels, on their way to work in the council, or the P and T or the ESB. Have to be there for eight. Early start. You'd swear it was Mondello.

There's a tink-clink-clink of jam-jars, as a forklift hits a rut and its cargo wobbles, that carries across the derelict roofs of the Market Yard and into the cracks and crevices of the town. On the sloping ground behind the roofs a sky-blue coat with a white paper hat moves across the sloping yard. Nolan, the floor manager, on the move, loading up for Tuam or Dubai. The bakers widow in her hanging mantilla passes on her way up to the convent. Royal-blue uniformed schoolgirls and a woman with a plastic bag stand under the canopy of Crofts shop entrance waiting for the bus. A white van pulls to a halt in front of Jimmy's and throws out newspapers and speeds off. Black flags adorn the telephone poles. Tim Shanley pushes his cart on Low street, sweeping. Swifts swoop from the eves of the thatched roof. A willie wagtail hops from the wall to the street and back to the wall again. Crows rise and settle on Jimmy's chimney pots. The Captain is thinking, One shot would get the two of them.

Father Duignan, your priest Melchizedek, late for mass, stops and knocks at the hall door of Kielty's to buy the Independent from a Republican publican, so he can read it while the nuns serve up his soft boiled egg, pinch of salt, butter, on their best china after a quick mass. And the master, an old republican with one eye, god knows why, some misadventure in his youth, or maybe active service, marches briskly down Low Street. Suit trousers creased and turned-up, black shoes shining, his felt fedora shading his eyes and his specially made black-rimmed glasses with one clear pane and one frosted pane hiding his bad eye, in to buy The Press off an old comrade.

Jimmy brings in the newspapers, and cuts their strings on top of the ice-cream fridge and looks at page three before the first farmer comes in for a large bottle of red lemonade that will be used to quench a thirst before noon in a dry meadow or at a reek the size of a house or a pike behind a byre or in a hay barn where he's forking hay to the roof off the buck-rake to the young lads tramping it down and wrestling. Across the square from Jimmy's, Shank Kilraine, the butcher, dreams of his red TR7 with it's pop-up headlamps.

Back inside, The Captain sits on his chair beside the table, pauses, and thinks of the day, before putting his feet into his shoes. He thinks of his egg joke, And how would you like your egg sir? With another one, please, if you don't mind. Ha, ha, ha! That's his prayers.

And I think of The Captain and the funny things that he'd say but now I know what he meant when he said, You only miss the shelter of the bush when its cut. I think again of my mother and her beautiful bright face and I know she'll write every week because she said she would.

24

THE FOLLOWING SUMMER

Jim Reynolds was building the internal walls on the extension to John Lowes—a big house the other side of Boyle. I was tending him. It was hot and I had my shirt off. I had to bring him blocks and keep him in mortar. I carried the blocks and stacked them four on edge and then four on edge crossways on top of that again—in stacks just the way he liked and positioned just where he liked—that way he never had to reach too far. Ned Smith said, Jim won't burst himself.

A yellow gas cylinder with a ring for boiling the kettle was placed in what was to be the kitchen when it was finished. I filled the burnt kettle from the hose and put it on the ring. Ned went round with a stump of a pencil and a bit of cement bag writing down what lads wanted for lunch. As he bounced out the gate on the tractor The Captain shouted, Ice creams, after him, but didn't think he'd heard.

I'd spent the previous Friday with Ned pulling down ceilings in the big old house. The lath and plaster ceilings crumbled when you touched them but then you had to pull all the rusty tacks that had held on the laths. When we had all the tacks pulled Ned said, The buck that put those in has no toothaches, meaning that he was long dead. I'd never heard that one before. Then I went out while Ned sprayed the rafters for dry-rot with his wool cap stuck in his mouth. We were black from head to toe with cobwebs and dust and I was blowing black stuff out of my nose for two days after.

When the kettle boiled I turned off the mixer. It felt like everything came alive when the rumble of the mixer died. You could hear birds chirping, leaves rustling, and it made you realise again that you were out in the country surrounded by green fields and big clean bullocks. Even the sun seemed brighter and felt hotter on my back. I noticed the fresh dark mortar between the light grey blocks. I noticed the sprinkling of fresh yellow saw-dust on the dry white concrete slab where Mick Raftery had cut shims. I saw where The Captain had thrown an empty red cigarette packet, half crumpled, on the pile of sweepings in the corner. I saw a brown stain of dried tea leaves fanning out across the white concrete floor, dregs thrown from a mug. I heard Dessie Moran whistling. I heard him drag the step ladder from one window to another as he prepped for painting. I heard the racing car whine of the electric plane from inside as Mick Raftery worked on hanging a bedroom door and I saw The Captain rustling through Ned Smith's lunch bag for a sandwich. I thought how it always felt strange moving from grey room to grey room when the walls were up but no roof on as yet.

I heard the sound of the kango inside the back door of the old house as Terry Mulvey kangoed out chasings in the floor for the plumber. Terry was fine and tall and bare chested and I could see the white concrete dust on his boots and clinging to the hairs of his strong brown legs. I leaned against the jamb of the door and felt the cool air from inside. I thought

I'd try out my new line on Terry and referring to the concrete floor I said, The buck that put that in has no toothaches. Terry half laughed and agreed, letting me know he understood and I felt like I had cracked a secret code. Then he said, Aye, and it's said as hard a grooms mickey. I'd never heard that one before either.

I wet the tea and one by one the lads arrived. I didn't have to call; they just knew, that when the mixer died it was time. Jim came back from the car carrying his dinged biscuit tin, with no lid, in one hand. Dessie Moran painter-decorator; speckled white overalls with the scraper in the side pocket, speckled hands, speckled black slip-on-going-to-mass shoes, served his time in London, up round the Holloway Road, Cricklewood Broadway, the Crown, Camden Town where the rough lie down, Fox and Hounds, Willesden Green, Piccadilly Circus, had one sandwich wrapped up in a loaf wrapper and the Sun newspaper tucked under his arm. I had held the triple extension for Dessie on the tech while he painted the fascias and soffits. He said his old legs couldn't take it, so he mixed the under coat and gloss together and finished it all in one coat and it looked toppin'—he had all the tricks. Dessie blew in his mug and turned it upside down and shook it and then held it out for tea. He found a spot in the shade and sat on a beer-barrel with his back to the grey wall. Ned said he was tasty and fierce particular.

I sat on a bag of cement and opened my lunch box—a biscuit tin full of corned beef sandwiches with brown bread and brown sauce. The bread had dried and the brown sauce and corned beef were warm. I had left it in the sun. I couldn't eat them. I wouldn't be doing that again.

The Captain didn't sit—he just stood drinking his tea and eating Ned Smith's sandwich. He said he wasn't that hungry and said he'd had three lamb cutlets for the breakfast in with

John Lowe. I could just imagine him sitting into that, not a bit embarrassed and asking for the bottle of chef sauce and a cut of white bread to clean the plate and a little hot drop just to wash it all down. He said all the big farmers on the good land up round Roscommon had lamb cutlets for breakfast every morning. I didn't know whether to believe him or not, but the land was better in Roscommon. It seemed to get better just after you crossed the bridge in Carrick and drove through the flood plain of the Shannon. But I knew other things about Roscommon farmers. I knew they all took night classes in welding in The Tech in Boyle in the winter and brought in their whole years supply of broken stuff to be welded by the teacher for nothing.

Terry Mulvey strode in with a loaf of bread, a packet of ham, six buns and a carton of milk and bounced up on a plank stretched between two forty gallon barrels. During the first week on the job Terry and I stopped in Knott's shop in Boyle on the way home to buy a pair of black shoes for his sisters wedding. He had Mister Knott running and pulling out shoes for him and he walked up and down the shop, long strides, several times in each pair, him in a pair of cut-off jeans and no shirt on. He even wanted to test them on the concrete footpath outside but Mister Knott wouldn't let him and he argued, looking down on a suited Mr. Knott, half his size, and said the soft carpet was a trick, that any pair of shoes would feel good on the soft carpet and a man couldn't tell rightly. I was in dread he'd buy nothing after putting Mister Knott through so much. When he eventually settled on a pair he haggled over the price and when he could get no more off he demanded that Mr. Knott throw in a spare pair of laces and a polish brush. Mr. Knott gave in. I think he wanted rid of him and I was glad to be out of there too. Mr. Knott then had to go and wrap all the shoes up again in their white paper, put them all back in their boxes and all the boxes back on the shelves.

Mick Raftery was the last to appear. He carried a lemonade crate and newspaper and had a lunch bag on his shoulder. He picked a spot in the sun and turned the crate upside down and laid the newspaper on it and then he moved two blocks over beside it to act as a low table. He took out a little baby-powers bottle of milk and a little plastic tub with teabags in it. I'd heard people talking about tea bags but I'd never seen them before. He took out another identical tub with sugar in it and then this unbreakable flask of boiling water. He laid them all out on his little table. Then he told the story again about how the flask fell out the side door of the Commer truck. He was taking the corner, out of Drumkeeran, heading for home, and it rolled the whole way down the main street and in through Wynne's shop-door and not a loss on it. Then everyone talked about this flask for a while and how good it was. The flask might have been a good idea but I still thought it would have been handier if he had made the tea with the milk and sugar all in the flask before he left the house like everyone else did.

Jim commented on Mick's new watch, a gold one with a red face and no hands. It was digital and the time came up in red numbers. He got it at an evening auction for two pound and he had to press a button on the side to get it to light up. It reminded me of the one the invisible man wore. Terry said that all that stuff at those auctions was made in Taiwan. Dessie said he thought it was good value and The Captain said he was robbed. As soon as Mick produced his spoon Jim wanted to borrow it. When Mick had his tea made he went back into the bag and took out a knife and fork wrapped in a paper napkin and a proper dinner plate with a salad on it wrapped in plastic. Cling film, he called it. I'd never heard of that before either. Then he produced a little plastic tub, like the others, with salad cream, and proceeded to apply it.

—We'll keep her, The Captain said, winking at Dessie, as Mick et with his head bent, letting on not to hear. Ned had said, Mick wasn't married a wet week.

—That'll only last so long, Dessie said, from behind the Sun. They're all great for the first month or two.

—Another month and you'll be like young Mulvey there, back to suppin' out of the milk carton, Jim piped in. That was more a dig at Dessie than Mick because Dessie caught Terry drinking directly from the carton we all used for our tea and was like a cut cat over it. At that, Mick began to go red and laugh and just said, Ah, fuck the lot o' ye. And everybody laughed.

—Did ye hear about Christy Martin, Terry started.

— No, well? The Captain said.

— They flew him back for the game on Sunday, the club paid for the flight, the whole lot.

—It's a great country, The Captain said.

—Tommy Reynolds went up to meet him at the airport, give him the full VIP treatment, the works, but he didn't recognise him getting off the plane. He was two stone heavier and had a perm in his hair.

—A perm won't be much addition come Sunday, The Captain said, mooching through Ned Smith's bag for another sandwich. 'Mooching,' that's what my mother would have called it. That's what she'd say when she'd catch The Captain and me red handed in the kitchen with all the presses open and drawers pulled out making roast beef sandwiches with salt and mustard on a Sunday evening.

—He's not going to go back either; they reckon he just took the free flight home.

—That'd be the cut of them Martin's all right, Jim said.

There's none of them any different. They're all split with the one axe.

—And what'll he do now, there's not much for him to do round here, Dessie asked.

—The bread roll, like the rest of us, Terry chirped from his perch.

—New York is the right place for him then, Jim said. It's a case of sink or swim in that town.

—No free dinners there, Dessie said.

—He could play football for New York, Mick said and everyone laughed. Then The Captain started going on again about Packy Mc Garthy and great Leitrim footballers of the fifties and I heard the tractor and gears grinding as it turned in off the road. The Captain heard it too, Good Jesus me clutch, he said. He was shaking his matchbox in one hand and swirling his tea in the bottom of his mug getting ready for the last sweet mouthful and a cigarette.

As the tractor approached I could see Ned was using his elbow to steer. He pulled up as close as he could and the sound of the tractor reverberated around the grey block rooms until he cut the engine and got out with three ice cream cones melting in a brown paper bag gripped in one hand.

—Suff'rin' Fuck, The Captain said, when he saw Ned and the three cones. The Captain had to take one and Ned gave me one and kept the third for himself.

—It's as hot as Turkey, Ned said, his scalp beginning to peel.

—Where's ours, Jim asked.

—You didn't ask for one, Ned answered, winking at me and licking his own as he lifted a block with one hand and left it down between me and Dessie and sat with his back to the cool wall. I hadn't asked for one either but Ned always thought of me. I was wondering what he'd be like when he discovered his sandwiches were gone. John Lowe the owner came out and wanted to talk to The Captain and he went off with his cone.

—I just heard below in the shop Art Quigley passed away, Ned said, looking at Mick. He was from over Mick's way.

—He's dead this fortnight, Mick said, with his mouth full.

—I never heard a word, said Ned.

—Well there you go, Mick said.

—He was supposed to have been a sight for the women, Ned said after a pause.

—Didn't he sell a woman for a chainsaw to a fella up at Gowel church, Jim cut in. Everyone laughed and then he said, He was supposed to have had an almighty weapon. Everyone laughed again.

—The man is dead leave him alone, Dessie said, and he wasn't laughing. I never knew whether to believe Jim or not. I knew Jim was liable to say or do anything since the day at Gaffney's he put on Missus Gaffney's nightgown and shower cap and did a lap of the house when The Captain was gone for paint.

Barney kept going, I heard he'd have no problem hopping it out. They said it was the length of twelve aul' pennies. Dessie got up and left. Jim was winking behind his back and jabbing his thumb in Dessie's direction, knowing he had him annoyed.

—Who counted out the pennies I wonder, Ned said beaming with a smile and elbowing me, his mouth all ice cream.

—Did you hear that, Dessie, Jim shouted through the door opening, twelve aul' pennies. That's the big ones with the hen and chickens on them. There was no response.

I thought that was the funniest thing I'd ever heard. Jim

was doing the calculation to work out the length. Ned Smith started rummaging through his bag for a sandwich and I was glad The Captain wasn't round to hear all this. Mick dipped in his bag again and took out one of those yoghurts and another spoon.

—She packed dessert an' all, Jim said, watching him.

—And my woman couldn't even put in a few blasted sandwiches, Ned said, pulling out his pipe and tobacco pouch. I didn't know whether I should tell him and was waiting for someone else to say something but nobody did.

—He was coming in at about fifteen inches, Jim said, as Dessie returned.

—What's that in new money, Ned said.

—Are ya still on about that?

—Fifteen inches, Jim said again.

D.F. just shook his head and sat down with the paper—shaking it and trying to fold it back on itself, a look of disdain on his face. I offered Ned one of my warm corned-beef sandwiches.

END